Millie's Steadfast Love

BOOK FIVE

of the
*A Life of Faith:
Millie Keith*
Series

Based on the beloved books by
Martha Finley

MCP
Mission City Press

Franklin, Tennessee

Book Five of the *A Life of Faith: Millie Keith* Series

Millie's Steadfast Love
Copyright © 2002, Mission City Press, Inc. All Rights Reserved.

Published by Mission City Press, Inc.

This book is based on the *Mildred Keith* novels written by Martha Finley and first published in 1876 by Dodd, Mead & Company.

Adaptation Written by:	Kersten Hamilton
Cover & Interior Design:	Richmond & Williams
Cover Photography:	Michelle Grisco Photography
Typesetting:	BookSetters

Unless otherwise indicated, all Scripture references are from the Holy Bible, New International Version (NIV). Copyright © 1973, 1978, 1984 by International Bible Society. Used by permission of Zondervan Publishing House, Grand Rapids, MI. All rights reserved.

Millie Keith and *A Life of Faith* are trademarks of Mission City Press, Inc.

For more information, write to Mission City Press at 202 Second Avenue South, Franklin, Tennessee 37064, or visit our Web Site at: **www.alifeoffaith.com.**

For a FREE catalog call 1-800-840-2641.

Library of Congress Catalog Card Number: 2002103829
Finley, Martha
      Millie's Steadfast Love
      Book Five of the *A Life of Faith: Millie Keith* Series
      Hardcover: ISBN-10: 1-928749-13-5
                      ISBN-13: 978-1-928749-13-4
      Softcover: ISBN-10: 1-928749-45-3
                      ISBN-13: 978-1-928749-45-5

Printed in the United States of America
4 5 6 7 8 — 12 11 10 09 08

DEDICATION

This book is
dedicated to
the memory of
MARTHA FINLEY
1828—1909

Martha Finley was a woman of God
clearly committed to advancing the cause of Christ
through stories of people who sought
to reflect Christian character in everyday life.
Although written in an era very different from ours,
her works still inspire both young and old
to seek to know and follow the living God.

—FOREWORD—

*I*n *Millie's Steadfast Love*, the fifth book of the "A Life of Faith: Millie Keith" series, you are invited to continue learning about the past as you grow in faith with Millie.

Our story resumes in the summer of 1837 as sixteen-year-old Millie travels home to Pleasant Plains with her father. She has spent almost a year at Roselands, the home of Horace Dinsmore, Sr., her mother's uncle. While there she turned down an offer of marriage, freed two slaves who did not belong to her, and was banished from Roselands by her southern relatives for the crime of slave-stealing. Sore at heart but eager to be home, Millie is about to find solace from an unexpected source—a friendship with a mysterious traveler, a Romani Gypsy.

∞ COMING TO AMERICA ∞

The face of America in 1838 was very different from the face of America today. The colonies, which had received their independence only sixty-two years before, had been founded and settled primarily by immigrants from England. To the north, Canada was colonized by France, and to the south were lands conquered by Spain. In addition to the English, Spanish, and French colonists, African men, women, and children were brought as slaves, as were the Romani people—sometimes known as Gypsies.

The Romani were a migratory people who had left India about a thousand years ago. They specialized in horse trading, metalwork, and entertainment. In the early 1300s the need for cheap labor to support growing feudal kingdoms led to the enslavement of the Romani across Europe. The

Romani had no country to claim them and no king to fight for their rights. Much like the Jews, the Romani were strangers wherever they went and were often accused of crimes or of spreading disease. The Code of Basil the Wolf of Moldavia, dated 1654, contained details of punishments and rules for Romani slaves. A law passed in 1547 by England's King Edward VI stated that Gypsies should be "branded with a V on their breast, and then enslaved for two years." If they tried to escape from this cruel treatment, they were branded with an S and made slaves for life. Spain, too, decreed in 1538 that Gypsies could be enslaved for life for trying to escape.

The first Romani to arrive in the New World were transported by Columbus to the Caribbean on his third voyage in 1498. Not all Romani people in the New World were slaves. Some sold themselves for a time as indentured servants to earn their berth on a ship. Others paid for their transport. But even in the Americas they faced centuries of persecution. A letter published in the *National Gazette* on May 19, 1834, reads: "There is yet another tribe, at or near Schenectady, called Yansers, although their patriarchal name is Kaiser. A gentleman appointed some years ago to some town office there, states that he found a charge of four pound ten shillings for whipping Yansers; the amount, being small, was allowed. A similar charge being brought the next year, he asked what in the name of goodness it meant? Behold, it was for chastising Gypsies whenever occasion presented, which was done with impunity and for some profit...it is supposed, by the best informed of my neighbors, that they came over with the early settlers in the German Valley...they are everywhere manufacturers of baskets, brooms and other wooden wares."

In the early 1820s, an influx of immigrants from Germany heralded the beginning of three great waves of immigration, which brought new people and new ideas to America, making it the most innovative and powerful nation on earth.

During the first wave, which lasted from 1820 to 1860, immigrants arrived from Great Britain, Ireland, and western Germany. The discovery of gold in 1848 in California brought Chinese and Latin American immigrants to the West Coast. There was a great deal of prejudice against people who looked and sounded different from the original colonists, but the land was so large there was room—and work—for all. The second wave, from 1860 to 1890, brought people from the Scandinavian nations.

In the third wave, 1890 to 1910, the majority of immigrants were from Austria, Hungary, Italy, and Russia. Today, people come from every nation on earth seeking a new life in the Land of the Free and the Home of the Brave—America. And each new wave of immigrants has brought its own wonderful contributions to this land.

∾ DISEASE FROM THE OLD WORLD ∾

Unfortunately, love for freedom and visions of a new life are not the only things Europeans brought across the ocean to America. In 1519, when Hernán Cortes started the conquest of Mexico, some of his men carried variola major—smallpox. This disease ravaged the Aztecs, making the conquest of their land much easier for the Spanish. It was only one of a long list of deadly diseases unwittingly imported to the New World: measles, influenza, mumps, typhus, cholera, plague, malaria, yellow fever, scarlet fever,

Foreword

whooping cough, and diphtheria all took a terrible toll of Native American lives. But smallpox was the most deadly. Epidemics of the disease had traveled through Europe for hundreds of years.

A major smallpox epidemic swept through the colonies of North America between 1776 and 1782, killing more colonial soldiers than all of the battles of the Revolutionary War combined. Smallpox, like measles, is much more severe if caught as an adult. And, as with measles, you can only get it once.

The British solders had survived the disease as children in England, but the Americans had no such protection. George Washington himself was immune, having almost died of pox when he was nineteen, but his soldiers were not. It threatened to destroy his army. There was a partial solution available. The men could be variolated, or intentionally infected, with what the doctors hoped was a mild form of the disease.

However, variolation was outlawed in many cities and towns because once a person was variolated, they did get a mild case of smallpox, and were contagious to others around them. While it was a good solution for the rich who could afford the expensive procedure and staying in bed for a month as they recovered, it was disastrous for the poor. The rich would travel to a town where variolation was legal, then return home to be cared for by their servants or slaves, thereby spreading the disease to the poor in their community, where it raged in the tenement houses and slave quarters, leaving death and agony in its wake. Pox was feared like the plague it was. The only safe way to contain the disease was to isolate the sufferers—to quarantine households or even whole towns. General Washington ordered the Continental Army to be variolated in 1776. Thousands of men were infected with the disease, and most recovered and were able to fight. If they had not been variolated, the Revolutionary War might have had a very different outcome. Both sides were aware of the risks of smallpox; the English had even considered using it as a weapon against the American army.

In Millie's day, it was still a feared and dreaded disease. This disease, which had such a huge impact on first the Native Americans and then the settlers, was finally wiped from the face of the earth in 1979 through an aggressive isolation and innoculation program run by the World Health Organization.

∽ THE MELTING POT ∾

Working together, facing sickness, privation, and the harsh realities of survival created a new type of society on the frontier. Good, caring neighbors were necessary for survival when a crop failure or a harsh winter could mean death. Every family contributed to the town and to the welfare of other families, and people from different backgrounds found that they had more similarities than differences. Think about the food you have eaten today. Who milked the cow or raised the grain or fruit that you have eaten? If you lived in frontier times, you would know where each bit of food on your table, and the clothes on your back, came from. They came from your own hard work, or that of your neighbors. Every member of the family from the youngest child to the oldest grandparent had a contribution to make. If you were a frontier girl like Millie, you would have been actively involved in helping your family to survive.

KEITH FAMILY TREE

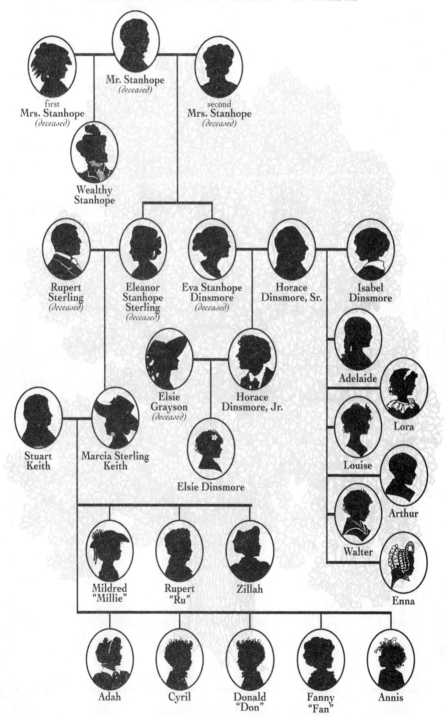

SETTING

$\mathscr{O}$ur story begins during the stagecoach journey of Millie Keith and her father from Philadelphia, Pennsylvania, to Lansdale, Ohio, on their way to their home in Pleasant Plains, Indiana.

CHARACTERS

∽ THE KEITH FAMILY ∽

Stuart Keith—the father of the Keith family and a respected attorney-at-law.

Marcia Keith—the mother of the Keith family and the step-niece of Aunt Wealthy Stanhope.

The Keith children:

>**Mildred Eleanor ("Millie")**—age 16
>**Rupert ("Ru")**—age 15
>**Zillah**—age 13
>**Adah**—age 12
>**Cyril** and **Donald ("Don")**—age 11, twin boys
>**Fanny ("Fan")**—age 9
>**Annis**—age 4

∽ LANSDALE, OHIO ∽

Wealthy Stanhope—Marcia's step-aunt who raised her from infancy, and step-aunt to Horace Dinsmore, Jr.

Mr. and Mrs. Hartley and their daughter **Beatrice ("Bea")** — longtime friends of the Keiths; Bea, **Camilla Stone,** and **Annabeth Jordan** were Millie's best friends since childhood.

∾ PLEASANT PLAINS, INDIANA ∾

The Lightcaps:

> **Rhoda Jane** — age 18; Millie's best friend in Pleasant Plains; she runs the local stagecoach way station along with her mother and brother.
>
> **Gordon** — age 20; he is the hostler and blacksmith at the local stagecoach station and a close friend of the Keiths.
>
> **Emmaretta** — age 12
>
> **Minerva ("Min")** — age 10

Reverend Matthew and Celestia Ann Lord — a local minister and his wife.

Dr. and Mrs. Chetwood — the town physician and his wife.

> **William ("Bill")** — age 18
>
> **Claudina** — age 17

Mr. and Mrs. Grange — the bank president and his wife.

> **Lucilla ("Lu")** — age 18
>
> **Teddy** — age 12

Mr. and Mrs. Monocker — the owner of the local mercantile store and his wife.

> **York** — age 20
>
> **Helen** — age 19

Mr. and Mrs. Ormsby — a local businessman and his wife.

> **Wallace** — age 19
>
> **Sally** — age 10

Mr. and Mrs. Roe — local farmers.

> **Beth** — age 18

Nicholas Ransquate and his wife **Damaris Drybread Ransquate** — friends of the Keiths.

Mrs. Prescott — a widowed neighbor.

Mrs. Prior — the landlady of the Union Hotel.

∞ OTHERS ∞

Gavriel Mikolaus ("Gavi") — a gypsy, age 20, with two younger siblings:

> **Jedidiah ("Jed")** — age 9
>
> **Jasmine ("Jaz")** — age 4

Mrs. Lyone and her son **Alexander** — stagecoach passengers.

Lyman Breeker — a stagecoach passenger.

Mr. Oakly — proprietor of the stagecoach way station in Oaklyville.

Ian and **Mary MacDonnell** — proprietors of a stagecoach way station.

George, Fenris Jones, and **Radly** — stagecoach drivers.

Charles Landreth — age 21; a friend of the Dinsmore family and nephew to the Landreths; he met Millie on her trip to Roselands and asked her to marry him.

CHAPTER

1

Heading Home

I have learned the secret of being content in any and every situation. . . . I can do everything through him who gives me strength.

PHILIPPIANS 4:12–13

A penny for your thoughts, Millie, mine."

Millie Keith glanced up at her father. "Are you sure you're not asking me that just to allow yourself time to catch your breath?" she teased. After a long day of sitting in a stagecoach, it was heavenly to be able to stretch her legs. Only nine months before, when she had made the journey from Pleasant Plains, Indiana, to her Uncle Horace Dinsmore's plantation in the South, the climb she had just completed would have been impossible. Her weakened lungs would have given out, leaving her racked with coughs. Millie took a deep breath of the sweet mid-June air. *I'm completely well,* she thought. *It's a miracle! The warm climate of the South contributed, of course. But didn't God create that climate?*

"I will pay a penny for your thoughts," Stuart Keith said with an exaggerated puff. "Slowing down would be worth at least a dime."

"Very well," Millie said, stopping to lean against a tree. Their journey toward home was proving to be long and arduous, but the countryside provided such beautiful land-scapes that even now, Millie was happy just to look out and take it all in. The hill behind the stagecoach way station was steep, but the view of the Tuscarora Mountains was spec-tacular. Purple twilight was already rising in the east. "I'll tell you my thoughts, and let you rest for free. I was think-ing that I cannot love someone more than Jesus does."

"That thought is worth much more than a penny," Stuart replied with a smile. "The *someone* you are thinking of wouldn't be Charles Landreth, would it?" he asked.

"Yes, Pappa."

"I wish I'd had a chance to meet this young man."

"You would have liked him," Millie said, taking her father's arm. The eight months that she had been with her cousins, the Dinsmores, on their plantation—the beautiful parties, the dresses and music, the fireflies rising on the soft southern nights, and Charles Landreth—were wrapped in a far-away, once-upon-a-time feeling. But not her memories of Luke and Laylie, the young slaves she had helped escape. Those memories were harsh and vivid, and they still made her cry. If she'd known the cost of helping her friends—losing the respect of her beloved Uncle Horace, being banished from Roselands forever—would she still have helped them escape? Aunt Isabel had accused her of theft and threatened to summon the law, even when Pappa had promised to pay for the slaves. Twelve hundred dollars! Millie hadn't known the amount until the captain presented her with a note bearing Isabel Dinsmore's seal. Her Aunt had sent it to the ship the night before their departure, instructing the captain to deliver it himself. Millie had to give it to her Pappa, of course. He'd looked grim as he folded it and put it in his pocket. "We'll pay it somehow," he'd said. "But until we do, those children won't truly be safe, even in New York."

Would I have helped if I'd known? Millie lifted her chin. *Yes. The answer is yes. Because that's what Jesus would have done. And I'm sure I made the right decision about Charles, too.* She'd lost count of the times she had dreamed of their last meeting.

"I do love you," she'd said to Charles. "With all my heart. But God's Word says that I can't marry you. I will do anything—even live without you—to prove to you that God's Word is true. You need His love much more than you need

mine." In her dream, Charles had explained that he did believe in Jesus. But the real-life Charles Landreth, the man Millie loved, had simply walked away.

Millie had kept to her cabin on the sea journey from Roselands to Philadelphia, worried that she would alarm the other passengers with her swollen eyes. But when they reached Philadelphia, she was determined to put the tears behind her. *Doesn't the Bible say to rejoice in all things? Well, it's not working. I feel about as joyful as a duck without a puddle.*

"How can He bear it?" Millie lifted her skirts to step over a fallen log. "How can Jesus bear loving people so much, when they don't love Him back?"

"I know His heart yearns after your Charles," Stuart said. "But you did the right thing. God's will is that Charles Landreth become not just a true gentleman, but also a true man of God. The best way you can help him do that is to be a true woman of God. And you are that, Millie. Now you must trust and wait."

Your Charles. Millie's cheeks burned at the words. *He's not mine, not really. I turned down his proposal not once, but three times. He could be proposing to some flirtatious Southern belle at this very moment. She's probably batting her eyelashes at him and saying yes . . .* Millie kicked a pinecone savagely. It hit a rock and bounced, missing Stuart by mere inches. "Sorry, Pappa. It's just . . . it's just that trusting is hard, but waiting is much harder—considering it might be forever."

Stuart patted her hand where it rested on his arm. "The trick to waiting is to find something else to do while you wait. I believe Jesus has a plan for you each and every day. Just ask Him, and He will give you an adventure."

"I'm not sure you know how adventuresome traveling with me can be, Pappa." Millie attempted a laugh. "Uncle

Horace said I was practically a menace. People burst into flames on trains, and boats hit sandbars. It was trouble wherever we went."

"Nonsense," Stuart said. "We have been traveling for two weeks, and our journey has been quite tame. Stagecoaches have no cinders to cause fires, and they very rarely run aground."

Changing the subject was not taking Millie's mind off her troubles. "Pappa? Do you think you could pray for me to love Charles less?"

"That I cannot do, Millie, because I know God does not want you to love him *less*. He wants you to love him *more*. No evil has ever come of loving the way God intended us to."

"But how can I know if I am loving Charles the way Jesus wants me to? It's too easy to confuse my wishes with His will."

"Love is patient," Stuart quoted from 1 Corinthians 13. "Love is kind. It does not envy, it does not boast, it is not proud." Millie joined in and they continued, "It is not rude, it is not self-seeking, it is not easily angered, it keeps no record of wrongs. Love does not delight in evil but rejoices with the truth. It always protects, always trusts, always hopes, always perseveres. Love never fails."

"I've read that passage many times in the last few weeks," sighed Millie.

"Don't just read it, Millie," Stuart said with deep conviction. "Hold your love up to that verse and see if there are any rips or tears in it. If there are, then ask Jesus to mend them."

"Will that keep my heart from breaking?" Millie asked with a sigh.

"No," Stuart said. "But it will keep it true to God, and that is more important. If we didn't love, we would never have broken hearts, but we wouldn't pray nearly as often or nearly as well, either."

"How did you get so wise, Pappa?"

"It is your Mamma's fault," he said with a wink. "She refused to have me any other way." His voice grew more solemn. "She will be so proud of the way you have grown in the Lord, Millie. And she will be proud of the way you have been faithful to God in your love for Charles."

Would Mamma be proud if she knew how hard it has been — how I struggled to figure out what God wanted me to do? How the feelings of my heart kept interfering with my loyalty to God? How afraid I am that I will never see Charles Landreth again?

"Some people are very easy to love," said Millie.

"Dinner's on!" The voice was surprisingly loud, considering the distance they had walked. They turned to look back at the way station. A stout figure on the porch stood waving her arms.

"And then there are others," Millie said with a sigh, "who make the task more difficult."

"Mrs. Lyone is not so bad," Stuart said, waving back at the woman.

Mrs. Lyone, an enormous woman whose pale face resembled a cheerful lump of dough, had boarded the stagecoach that very morning. She was traveling to Lansdale, Ohio, with her equally large son, Alexander. She had instantly assumed an uncomfortably maternal stance toward Millie and insisted on seating her next to Alexander at every opportunity.

"May I escort you to dinner, my dear?" Stuart asked with a bow.

Millie's Steadfast Love

"I suppose we must," Millie said, taking her father's arm. As they started back down the hill to the station, Millie thought about the previous way stations along their route. They'd come in every size and description. Some were hotels and others were merely homes that offered food and sometimes rooms for the guests. The one where they were currently stopped could best be described as a disaster. Mr. Oakly, the proprietor, had been in the right place at the right time, and so the stagecoach company had paid him to convert his home into a way station. With the arrival of the stagecoach line, he had declared the place a town—Oaklyville—and put up a sign, naming himself mayor, sheriff, and justice of the peace. They were all elected offices, he explained, and since he was the only voter, he had no choice but to elect himself. "I never could stand political debates," he said, "so it's just as well there's no one to run against me!"

Millie and Stuart made their way back down the hill, past the corral, and up the steps.

"I hope you haven't been walking in damp grass," Mrs. Lyone said as Stuart seated Millie in the dining room of the one and only home in Oaklyville. "Damp shoes are bad for the health," she continued. "Alexander is a fortress of vigor and vitality, but damp shoes will have him sneezing in a moment's time! I don't know that it's wise to traipse about in the bushes."

The boy looked down at his plate and sniffled. He was suffering from a slight cold, attested to by his runny nose and red eyes. He started to wipe his nose on his sleeve, looked quickly at his mother, and reached for a napkin, apparently not carrying a handkerchief. Millie pretended not to notice.

8

The food—bread and butter, baked potatoes, ham, and cabbage slaw—was plentiful, if not particularly tasty, and if the silverware was spotted and the tablecloth of questionable color, the smudges on the lantern's mantle kept the light from being too revealing.

Millie had learned to look for the bright spots and blessings—even in such a place as this. She counted among today's blessings George, the stagecoach driver. He had been the most pleasant driver they had encountered yet on their cross-country journey.

"I hope you folks had a good ride today," he said, hanging his coiled whip on the back of his chair before he sat down.

"It was very smooth," Stuart assured him.

"That's good to hear. The boss does like a satisfied customer!"

Millie smiled. Many stagecoach drivers were arrogant, prone to showing off and bragging. Of course it did take a great deal of strength and skill to command a team of four or six horses, handling a separate set of reins for each.

"We are certainly satisfied," Mrs. Lyone beamed at him. "But tell me, doesn't it weigh heavily on you? Your passengers' lives are in your hands. Racing through darkness and storms. I don't know how you do it!"

"Darkness and storms are nothing, ma'am," George said, taking a bite of ham. "Now the trails up the mountain tomorrow," he pointed with his fork, "that's where you need a *driver*. One mistake, and—"

"Oh, please! I am deathly afraid of heights," Mrs. Lyone said to George with a grimace. "I cannot bear to think of it ahead of time."

"Heights are nothing to worry about," he said confidently. "It's the falling off that kills you."

"Really?" said Millie. "I thought it was the landing." Stuart raised his eyebrows, but Mrs. Lyone's gasp and the twang of the Holy Spirit in Millie's heart were chastisement enough. *Forgive me, Lord,* Millie prayed quickly.

"You do have a point," George said. "But don't you worry none, ma'am. There's a reason we get the best table at every stop and the biggest piece of pie!" He held his hands up and spread his fingers wide. "We've got magic in our hands."

Alexander spread his hands. "I . . . I'd like to try it," he said. "You control each horse with its own set of reins, I understand."

"Start out driving one team just to learn," George said. "A driver controls two to three horses with each hand. Goin' up the mountain, control is mighty important. Team don't turn all at once on those sharp corners, no sir! You've got to turn your leaders, then your swings, and then your wheelers, and each pair just right. If they get tangled, they'll overturn the stagecoach. A driver has to have strong hands and good timing."

Mrs. Lyone fanned herself furiously. "Oh, dear."

"Sorry, ma'am. I didn't mean to fluster you. Drivers on this line don't roll their coaches. Let me tell you about the Higglesfoot and Wiggens race." He entertained them through the meal and into the evening with tales of Indian raids, road agents, and wild races between stagecoach drivers.

"I cannot take any more!" Mrs. Lyone said at last, covering her ears with plump pink hands. "I won't be able to sleep for fear of savages creeping up on us."

Mr. Oakly took this as a hint and, picking up the dim lamp from the table, offered to show the guests to their rooms. George bid them all goodnight, saying he would sleep in the stagecoach.

Mr. Oakly only had two guest rooms, so travelers were split up according to gender rather than relation. Stuart and Alexander were given the smaller room, and Millie and Mrs. Lyone were led to "the leddies room," a large, dingy room with an odd contraption of mixed and matched bedposts with a lumpy mattress and a few thin blankets. There was also a chair and a desk with an oil lamp on it, which Mr. Oakly kindly lit before he left them. The single gleam of color was a brass spittoon in the corner. The sour-sweet smell of chewing tobacco juice indicated that the spittoon was at least partially full, but even more distressing was the large tobacco juice stain still evident on one pillow slip. Mrs. Lyone turned the pillow over and patted it. "He's not washing the linen any more than he has to, is he?" She looked at the spittoon, and then at the small tin box Millie had pulled from her bag. "Do you use tobacco, dear?"

"No," Millie said, hoping that was also true of Mrs. Lyone. It was unsettling to see people spit the brown juice across a room when their aim was good, and nothing short of horrifying when it was not.

"That's good," Mrs. Lyone said. "A lady should never use tobacco, at least not until she reaches the age of fifty." She picked up the spittoon, put it in the hall, and closed the door before lowering herself onto the bed. "If you don't chew, then . . .?" She eyed the box Millie had placed by her Bible.

"That's rather personal," Millie said. Then realizing that it had sounded snippy, Millie added, "It's just a keepsake from my visit to my uncle's plantation." The box held a single dried rose from the last bouquet Charles had given her.

"Oh," Mrs. Lyone said, without much interest. She sighed, "I could sleep through the angel Gabriel's trumpet tonight—I'm that tired. Just help me with my shoes, dear." She held up one stout leg.

Millie looked at the boot for just one second before she stepped forward. *Thank You for giving me a chance to help her, Lord,* she prayed as she grasped the boot, unbuttoned it, and pulled it off.

"Ahhhhhh!" Mrs. Lyone said, wiggling her toes. She offered the other foot, and Millie repeated the procedure.

"Your mother is a lucky one," the woman said, giving Millie a sideways look. "My Alexander is a jewel, a real gem, but I have always yearned for a daughter. May heaven grant me one when Alexander marries. And whoever he marries will be getting a bargain, I can tell you." She sighed heavily. "Help me with my corset, won't you? I can barely breathe." Millie loosened the laces so that Mrs. Lyone could wiggle out of it. "What exquisite bliss it is to be free from that device," Mrs. Lyone said with a sigh as she collapsed upon the bed.

"Why do you wear it then?" Millie asked.

"Fashion is a cruel dictator, dear," the woman said. "One who pinches our toes, cracks our ribs, and insists that we smile pleasantly all the while."

Millie slipped her own nightgown on over her head before she took off her dress, petticoats, and camisole.

"You don't wear a corset, do you? Well, I had a figure too in my day," said the woman.

Millie felt herself blushing as she folded her clothes and put them in her bag. "If you don't mind the lamp being on a little longer," Millie said, "I would like to read my Bible."

"Lord bless you, dear. Won't you read aloud? My own mister used to read me a bit of the Good Book at the end of

the day before he went on to glory." She punched the lumpy mattress several times, lay down and wallowed from side to side a bit, and then pulled the blankets up to her chin.

Millie had just started the third chapter of the book of John when a soft snore informed her that her listener was no longer paying attention. She finished her reading aloud anyway. *Perhaps the words will settle into Mrs. Lyone's dreams, reminding her of her mister.*

When Millie was finished, she damped the light, pulled back the covers, and slid under the sheets. The pillow smelled slightly sour, reminding her of the tobacco juice from the corner. Millie turned it over, and found to her dismay that the underside was even worse. There the tobacco stains were crusty. She dropped it over the side of the bed.

Mrs. Lyone had subdued the bedding so completely that the entire bed—posts and all—bowed to her weight, sagging toward her from all points. Even the bedposts seemed to give in to her might. Millie tried to balance herself on the edge, but the moment she relaxed, she started to roll downhill. She turned onto her stomach, one leg and one arm hanging over the edge of the bed to hold her in place.

Lord, I am truly thankful for a bed, and the discomfort may take my mind off Charles. Sleep! she commanded herself. *Don't think about him. Don't think about the way he smiles.*

Well, that isn't working. All right then, I will think about him. Lord, I don't want to love Charles right now. But since I do love him, help me to love him the right way. Your way. Help him to become a Christian, a true man of God. And help me to be patient. Help me to bear all things, hope all things, and endure all things. Most of all, Lord, keep my heart faithful to You . . .

Suddenly something tickled along Millie's leg under the covers. Her eyes flew open. *Is there a spider in this bed?* The tickle came again and Millie jumped up, brushing wildly at her nightgown and stubbing her toe on the leg of the table as she fumbled for a match.

"What is it?" Mrs. Lyone mumbled, rolling over.

"I felt something moving in the bed!" Millie said. "I didn't mean to wake you, but I thought it might be a spider. Ouch!" She flipped her hand as the flame reached her fingers, and the match went out. Millie fumbled in the dark for another, this time using it to light the lamp.

Mrs. Lyone heaved herself up. "I can't abide spiders," she grumbled. "Let's just have a look." They pulled the sheets down, and Millie held the lamp close. Something was moving—several somethings, in fact. Fat, flesh-colored bugs, some as large as the nail of her little finger.

"Eeeek!" Mrs. Lyone squealed, leaping up. Millie backed into the corner as the woman proceeded to dance and flail, slapping her legs and running in place, finally settling into a prolonged jiggle, punctuated by the occasional stomp and squeak.

"What are they?" Millie asked.

"Bedbugs!" Mrs. Lyone said. "I was too tired to feel the little beasts crawling." Millie covered her mouth in horror. "They suck your blood," Mrs. Lyone continued. "They creep into the mattress to hide. Their bites itch worse than mosquito bumps, too. Once you get bedbugs, the only cure is to burn the mattress and the bed frame. Even that won't help sometimes. The little devils hide in the walls and floor."

Millie examined her clothes as carefully as she could in the lamplight, and then pulled on her petticoats, camisole, and dress. She went next door to Stuart's room and knocked softly. The door opened to reveal Stuart still dressed, and Alexander perched on the side of the bed.

"Get up, Alexander," Mrs. Lyone said as she brushed past Millie and pushed her way boldly into the room. "There's bedbugs in the works." She pulled back the covers while Millie held the lamp close. Bugs scurried for the dark folds of fabric.

"I think we will sit up in the dining room tonight," Stuart said, picking up his unopened bag from the dressing table.

They found George still in the dining room, finishing off the pot of coffee that had been brewed for dinner.

"What got you folks up?" he asked. "Old Oakly's gone on to bed."

"Bedbugs, that's what!" Mrs. Lyone grumped. "They should change the name of this place to Bugtussle."

"Stayed in Bugtussle once," the stagecoach driver announced. "Bugtussle, Louisiana. It was a right nice place," he said, rising to leave. "Goodnight." He turned his cup bottom up on the saucer, and went outside.

A very uncomfortable night was had by all, sitting on the hard benches of the dining room. Alexander was the only one who managed a few winks. His snore, Millie noted, was identical to his mother's.

⁓

Millie felt decidedly rumpled and out of sorts when morning came. Not only had she had little, if any, sleep, but she had worn her travel clothes all night.

"Pappa," she whispered, as dawn began to creep into the sky, "will you guard the door of the storage room off the kitchen so I may change?" Mrs. Lyone's eyes followed her as she left the room, but the woman didn't move for fear of waking Alexander, who leaned against her shoulder.

Millie's Steadfast Love

Millie carried the stub of a candle into the storage closet with her. Most of her clothes were in the trunks on the stagecoach, but she had one dress in her carpetbag—the one she had been planning to wear on her arrival in Pleasant Plains—folded neatly and wrapped in brown paper to keep it from wrinkling. Millie set the candle on a shelf beside a tin of flour and pulled the dress from her bag. It was her favorite gown—a lovely dove gray with periwinkle trim and a matching periwinkle cap that framed her face. French lace pantalets that fell in ruffled cascades over her high-top shoes completed the outfit. She did the best she could with her hair, considering she had no mirror. By the time she had set the cap on her head, Pappa was knocking at the door.

"Mr. Oakly is requesting the use of his storage room," Stuart said. "I believe he wants to start breakfast."

Millie quickly shoved her old dress into the bag, gave her hair one last pat, and opened the door.

" 'Bout time," Mr. Oakly grumbled.

"You look very lovely," Stuart said, offering his arm. Millie certainly felt better. Isabel Dinsmore had many bad traits, but she did have excellent taste in clothes, and Millie had learned quite a lot by watching her during the months at Uncle Horace's. A fresh dress made all the difference in facing the day.

"Mornin', folks," George called cheerfully when he came in just after dawn. "You're all up bright and early."

"We haven't had a wink of sleep," Mrs. Lyone sighed. "I hope you fared better."

"Slept like a child. Just tossed the mail bags on the floor of the stagecoach, grabbed a blanket, and climbed right on top of them."

"What time will we be leaving?" Millie asked, thinking that the padded seat of the stagecoach would afford more comfort than the dining room benches.

"Can't tell you that," the driver said. "I'm not taking you on. Line splits here, and I go on north. Radly's coming along to take you over the mountain. I'm surprised he didn't come last night." He glanced at Mrs. Lyone and lowered his voice. "Lots of folks prefer going over at nighttime. They can't see that way." He raised his voice again when Mrs. Lyone glanced at them. "He's about to get his pay docked, I guess. Company's real strict about being on time and ready to go. I hope that's breakfast I smell, 'cause I need to be movin' on." He wandered into the kitchen.

He was no more than out of sight when they heard a stage horn blast. Stepping to the window that overlooked the barnyard, Millie saw the stagecoach lurch to a stop. The horses had obviously been driven hard, as they were flecked with sweat. It was a beautiful stagecoach, the body in a rich vermilion with yellow running gear, but smaller than the one they had arrived in.

The door flew open and a boy of perhaps fifteen jumped out. He ran immediately to the horses and started pulling the harness off. The driver, a large, shaggy man, took his time climbing down from the box. Dismounting from his high seat at the front of the stagecoach was a little difficult for him, as he had a peg leg. He apparently had it fastened to the brake lever in some way, because he grasped it with his hands, pulled it up, and then swung it over the side of the coach. This feat accomplished, he jumped heavily to the ground and stumped past the boy, who didn't look up from his work. *Is the boy not a passenger then?* Millie wondered. The stagecoach door opened again, and a tall, elderly gentleman stepped down and turned to help two small children—a boy who looked to be about nine years old and a young girl who looked about four or five—down the narrow step to the ground.

"Did I hear a horn?" George had returned, a cup of coffee in his hand. "That would be Radly, here to take you folks on."

"Radly will not be driving," a voice growled. "I will." Millie forced herself not to stare as he thumped across the wooden floor.

"Fenris Jones," George said, shaking his head. "Well I'll be switched! Did they let you drive again? I thought you was dead—or at least busted down to bullwhacker."

CHAPTER

2

Mysterious
Passengers

*She opens her arms to the poor
and extends her hands to
the needy.*

PROVERBS 31:20

hat little of the man's face Millie could see above his whiskers grew red with anger. "Do I look dead?" he blurted out.

"Not completely." George scratched his head. "But there's a bit less of you than there was the last time we met."

The red deepened to purple, and Millie was sure the man was gritting his teeth.

"Let's just get these folks' trunks moved so's you can be on your way," George suggested.

Stuart accompanied them, though whether to help with the trunks or prevent a fight Millie was unsure.

Just as the men were leaving, the elderly gentleman passenger ushered the children in the door. The pair looked warily at the pegged-leg driver, edged past him, and scooted toward a bench. They were amazingly handsome little children with dark, mysterious eyes and thick lashes. The little girl wore ribbons on each of her two thick braids, but no bonnet.

"Hello." Her eyes twinkled as she spoke to Millie and gave a little curtsy. "My name's Jasmine. Jasmine Amaia Mikolaus." She pronounced each syllable carefully.

"That's enough, Jaz," the boy said, grabbing her shoulder. "Sorry to bother you, miss."

"It is certainly no bother," Millie said, smiling at the child. "I'm Millie Keith. Your grandchildren seem well mannered, sir," she said, extending her smile to the older gentleman.

"Lyman Breeker," he said, lifting his hat. "Pleased to meet you, miss, but Jedidiah and Jaz are none of mine."

Millie looked at the boy in surprise. *Is he traveling alone with his sister?* "Would you like to go wash up before breakfast?" Millie asked. "I'm just on my way to do so now," finished Millie, smiling at the little girl.

"No," Jedidiah said protectively, "she's not dirty."

Millie went to the back porch where Mr. Oakly had set out a basin, soap, and towels. The older boy from the stagecoach was just rolling down his sleeves after washing his hands. He flashed Millie a startled look, then pulled his cap down. He was obviously the brother of the two children inside. He had the same fine features and incredible, dark onyx-colored eyes. His baggy trousers were held up with suspenders, and his shirt, which showed wear at the cuffs and collar, had been boiled white.

"I asked your brother and sister to come out and wash," Millie said with a smile. "But your brother seems to be wary of strangers." The boy nodded, tugging at the brim of his cap as he went past. There was just a hint of a shuffle in his walk, as if the boots on his feet were a few sizes too big. Mr. Oakly arrived with a scowl on his face and a fresh towel in his hand.

"Thought you might need this," he said. "I wouldn't ask you to use a towel after that gypsy touched it."

"The boy didn't do any harm to the towel. He appears to have been very neat," Millie remarked in the boy's defense.

"Humph," Mr. Oakly said. "I know his kind, know them by sight. Gypsies and tinkers. They'll steal you blind . . . and him and those youngsters traveling alone by stagecoach. Why, where do you think they got tickets? Lifted 'em off some honest citizens, I'll wager. Did he take my soap?"

Millie looked down at the dish. "Your soap appears to be safe. Why would you think that boy was a gypsy?"

"The horses," Mr. Oakly said in a half-whisper. "He was talking to them."

"Lots of people talk to their horses," Millie said. "I do it myself."

"Maybe so, miss, but when gypsies talk their yibber-yabber, the dumb beasts listen. Those horses understood what he was saying."

"Surely he was being kind to the animals, and that shows a good heart," responded Millie.

"They may be kind to animals, but they'll knife you in the back quick as they can blink those black eyes. They're gypsies, I tell you, full of tricks and black magic." He set the towel down, picked up the one the boy had used with two fingers, and spat a stream of brown tobacco juice into the corner of the porch. "Speaking as mayor of this here town, I don't like 'em around. Not one bit." He carried the towel gingerly away.

Millie shook her head, then took her time straightening her hair and washing her hands and face.

Mr. Oakly may have been opinionated as mayor, but he was merely the cook when Millie re-entered the dining hall—a cook in a greasy apron at that—busily placing bowls on the table. Stuart seated Millie, and then pulled a chair out for Jaz. She giggled up at him as she climbed into it.

Mr. Oakly glared at the older boy's cap. The cap remained firmly on his head, but the boy narrowed his eyes and the cook looked away quickly, reaching for the salt shaker. He made a show of shaking salt into the gruel, then with a glance at the boy, gave one toss over his shoulder to ward off evil.

"I'm Stuart Keith," Stuart said, holding out his hand to the boy. The boy hesitantly reached for Stuart's hand.

"Gavi," he said in an odd, husky voice. "Gavi Mikolaus." He released Stuart's hand, then lowered his eyes.

Mr. Oakly ladled a thick, gray glob of gruel into the bowl in front of Millie. "Eat up, young lady," he said. "It's a long way to the next station." A black dot bobbed to the surface of the goo. *I hope that's a raisin*, thought Millie. She was somewhat startled when the children grabbed their spoons before the porridge hit their bowls.

Stuart had bowed his head for a blessing, but Mr. Breeker said, "Pray after the meal, sir. There is no time for that nicety, I assure you!" Mrs. Lyone was looking uncertainly at the mess in her bowl, but Alexander had taken Mr. Oakly's advice and was eating his breakfast. Stuart looked at Millie and shrugged. They both quietly bowed their heads for grace, and Millie settled her napkin on her lap. She had taken no more than two bites when the horn blew outside the door.

"We have to go, Jed, Jaz," Gavi said. "He'll leave us if we don't hurry."

"Surely not!" Mrs. Lyone said. "We have hardly begun our meal."

"You wonderin' what happened to ole Fenris's leg?" asked George. "Folks say it fell asleep and he hadn't no patience to wait for it to wake up, so he lopped it off and left it," he continued, shaking his head.

"That is a ridiculous story," Mrs. Lyone sniffed. "I'm sure you are making it up."

"Well, now, I did make it up," George said. "But I wouldn't put it past him."

Gavi had been gathering his things as they spoke. "Let's go," he said, taking Jaz's hand. They started for the door.

" 'Fraid the youngster's right," Mr. Breeker said calmly. "Fenris has been trying to get rid of his passengers all along.

Thinks he's a real Jehu, driving fast and furious. Glad this is the end of the line for me. I don't think I could take much more of that man, and I'm a little old to whip him."

Millie looked at her father. He pressed his lips together firmly, then nodded. "We'd better go," he said. "I don't want to wait for the next stagecoach. I have been away from my wife quite long enough."

"What do you mean this is the end of the line for you?" Mr. Oakly said to Mr. Breeker as they stood up. "You can't stay in this town. Think what it would do to the elections. It would be plumb un-American." They were arguing politics as the Keiths went out the door.

By the time they reached the stagecoach steps, Fenris Jones had lost all patience. He lifted his whip, but before it could crack, Gavi put his fingers to his lips and produced a piercing whistle. The horses' ears turned toward him, and then lowered their heads. The whip cracked above their backs, but they did not move.

Fenris Jones whirled to look at Gavi, whip still in hand. "You do that to my team again," he said, "and I will use this on you, boy."

"Hold your horses, man!" Stuart said, stepping between them. "Just let the ladies settle themselves and we will be on our way."

Jones's face flushed purple with anger, and he rubbed his left shoulder.

"Are you in pain?" Stuart asked.

"Just get in the coach," the man said gruffly, gritting his teeth. Stuart helped Mrs. Lyone to board, and then picked up Jaz and put her in the stagecoach. She giggled and kicked her little black boots as he lifted her in. Her brothers followed and then Millie. The stagecoach they had arrived in the day before had seats for nine passengers, but this one could seat only six. Mrs. Lyone had taken the rear seat for herself and her son. Jedidiah had squeezed onto that seat as well, with Jaz on his lap. Gavi had scooted to the far corner of the front seat. Millie glanced in surprise at Alexander. Social custom called for a gentleman to give up his seat for a lady, taking the less desirable front seat, as riding backwards could be unsettling to the equilibrium.

"Alexander has a delicate stomach," Mrs. Lyone explained with a slight flush. "He *has* to sit in the back seat." A slight green tinge did seem to be creeping up the young man's face.

"Don't worry," Millie said kindly. "I am blessed with an iron constitution and do not mind riding backwards in the least." She took the window seat, allowing her father to take the middle seat between herself and Gavi. Stuart had just enough time to sit down before the coach took off with a jolt.

Gavi pulled a small doll from the pocket of his coat and handed it to Jaz, who seemed perfectly happy chattering to it, holding it up to see out the window, rocking it in her arms, and singing lullabies as she stroked its soft hair.

Conversation covered all subjects polite company might mention on a stagecoach, and when it dwindled, Stuart unfolded the paper he had brought with him, reading the second page with interest. Millie was sure he had read every word at least six times, as he had purchased it a week ago, but holding it in front of his face did afford some privacy in the cramped surroundings. Millie had a stack of magazines in her carpetbag through which she was pursuing a serial story, *The Posthumous Papers of the Pickwick Club*, by a new writer named Charles Dickens. She had just opened to the third installment when Mrs. Lyone, who had apparently not brought any reading material, cleared her throat.

"Mr. Keith," Mrs. Lyone said in a businesslike way, "may I ask your profession?"

"I profess to be a Christian," Stuart said, smiling as he laid his paper down. "But if you would like to know what I do for a living, I practice law."

"A lawyer!" Mrs. Lyone exclaimed once she figured out what he was saying. "How marvelous! You must be extremely intelligent. I would like to ask your opinion if you don't mind."

"About a legal matter?"

"Of a sort. I have been considering . . ." and here she glanced meaningfully at Millie, "the wisdom of arranged marriages." Millie fixed her gaze on the page, afraid to meet her father's eyes for fear of bursting out laughing. "What are your views?" Mrs. Lyone continued. "I myself think that if it was good enough for our grandmothers, and even for people in Bible times, it should be good enough for us. I don't know that young people are to be trusted in such matters."

Stuart examined her gravely. "That is a serious question. I don't think we are ever old enough or wise enough to decide these things completely for ourselves," he said. "I would say the young person who was willing to pray for wisdom and consider the advice of elders has an advantage."

"What do you think, Mr. Mikolaus? I would certainly like a young man's opinion on the subject. I have quite a disagreement over this with my son Alexander."

Gavi studied Alexander's pale face for a moment, and then turned his attention to Mrs. Lyone. "I think," he said, "that people should mind their own business." He pulled his cap down over his eyes, folded his arms, and stretched his legs out in front of him, obviously going to sleep. Millie used her handkerchief to hide a smile.

"Well!" said Mrs. Lyone. "Some people!" She looked around for reinforcements, but Stuart had buried his nose in a paper again. Millie looked away quickly, deciding to be fascinated by the scenery, which was passing at a snail's pace because they were making their way up a steep hillside. The road was narrow and winding, but the stagecoach clung to the cliffs, moving slowly enough for a fat horsefly to buzz in and out of the open window, pursuing them with the intent of landing on Mrs. Lyone's nose.

Conversation again dwindled to silence, with Stuart reading his paper and the others dozing or gazing out the window. The motion of the coach and the lack of sleep the night before eventually overcame both the Lyones. Their soft snores were almost a lullaby, with rhythm kept by the horses' hooves. Jaz was having a hard time keeping still, needing room to stretch her little legs. She moved between her brothers' laps, growing grumpy as the morning wore on.

Millie took a length of yarn from her basket and made a cat's cradle. The little girl leaned toward her. "Would you like to learn how to make one?" Millie asked. Jaz looked to Gavi for permission. He nodded, and she squeezed past Mrs. Lyone's knees and crawled up onto Millie's lap. They spent half an hour playing cat's cradle and finger rhymes before the child started to fidget.

"Gavi," she said in a loud whisper. "I've got to go, really, really bad."

"You've got to hold it this time," her brother said, looking embarrassed. "You know he won't stop."

"Nonsense!" Stuart said, vigorously thumping on the top of the stagecoach with his fist. The stagecoach didn't slow at all. Stuart frowned. "Will you trade places with me, Millie?" They managed to switch seats, and Stuart leaned out the window.

"Mr. Jones!" he called more loudly. "We have a young lady in some distress here. Will you please stop?" The stagecoach continued on its laborious way up the hill. "Hold this, my dear," Stuart said, handing his hat to Millie. "Perhaps he's hard of hearing."

"Perhaps he's rotten mean," Jedidiah said. Stuart didn't answer as he swung the door open and, gripping the frame, leaned out to speak with the driver.

"I'm afraid you did not hear," he spoke louder. "We have a young lady in distress. We need to stop for a few moments." There was a snarled reply, but still the stage-coach did not slow down.

"I am quite happy to come up and assist you in applying the brake," Stuart said firmly. Millie was sure that if they had not been going uphill, the driver would have whipped the horses into a run. As it was, he had no choice but to pull aside.

Stuart helped Jaz from the stagecoach, and her brother took her into the bushes. The other passengers took the opportunity to stretch their legs.

"I'm behind schedule already," Fenris Jones said angrily. "You folks are going to have to make the time up at the next station." The coach was soon loaded again, the passengers' moods all improved by the stop, even if Fenris was red-faced with rage at the delay.

It was past one in the afternoon when the tired team dragged into a stable yard. The passengers were more than ready for their noon meal. The station was a lovely home built of logs and stone, with large glass windows that looked out over the valley and a wide, well-swept porch. Even Mrs. Lyone was impressed with the beauty of the view.

"Can we take a walk, Pappa?" Millie asked.

"Yes, and let's invite Jaz along," Stuart said, winking. "She might enjoy stretching her legs."

"We're not going to be here long enough for a walk," Mr. Jones growled. "So don't wander off, or you'll be left. They knew we were coming, so get in and eat and get it over with so's we can be on our way."

Gavi narrowed his eyes at the driver, who just walked away.

"Is your brother putting an evil eye on the driver?" Mrs. Lyone asked.

"My brother? Oh, Gavi." Jedidiah laughed nervously. "Mamma said that when you don't love someone one bit, you have to try to see them like Jesus would. It's a hard thing to do. Even Mamma has to squint sometimes."

Millie looked at the boy in surprise. It sounded very much like something her Aunt Wealthy had told her once. "Your mamma sounds like a very wise person. Is she waiting for you at your journey's end?"

The boy took a step back, but Gavi took his hand. "Yes," Gavi spoke quickly. "She'll be waiting for us. Come on, Jed."

Millie shook her head as they walked away. "I think they are in trouble, Pappa. Somewhere, somehow, they are in trouble."

Stuart nodded his head. "I have been thinking the same thing."

"I wish we could help," Millie said.

"I am afraid you are becoming an adventurer, just like your Aunt Wealthy."

"Don't pretend you haven't been trying to figure out what their trouble is!" said Millie.

"Of course I have," he said with a wink. "Lord," he spread his arms and looked up into the blue. "You said that wherever two are agreed in prayer, You would be there. My adventuresome daughter and I would like to present ourselves for Your service." His face grew solemn. "I don't know what their trouble is, Lord, but if we can be Your hands or Your messengers for these children, please let us."

"Amen," Millie agreed.

CHAPTER

3

A Wild Ride

Save us and help us with your right hand, that those you love may be delivered.

PSALM 108:6

A Wild Ride

*T*his way station was significantly better than the one at Oaklyville. Besides a handsome home, it had a corral and two barns for the horses.

"Come in, come in," a tall, thin woman called from the door. "The food is all ready, and I'm sure you are hungry."

"Madam," Stuart said with a smile. "I am not hungry. I am famished!" He held the door as Millie stepped inside.

"Ian MacDonnell." A gentleman whose red hair was peppered with gray extended his hand to Stuart. "And this is my wife, Mary." The two greeted each guest as if they were old friends and showed them into the parlor. The room was rustic but lovely, with a huge stone fireplace surrounded by heads of animals Millie had only read about. Most impressive of all was the tiger skin stretched across the floor, its mouth opened in a bare-fanged snarl.

Jaz squatted by its head. "Poor kitty," she said.

"Now don't be too sympathetic," Mr. MacDonnell said. "That cat was a bad one in his day. Lived in the hill country of India, and he liked to eat little girls. Had to put a stop to that, didn't I?"

"You shot the beast yourself?" Mrs. Lyone asked, still staring at the tiger skin. "You must be terribly brave."

"I like to pretend to be," the innkeeper laughed. "But the truth is, I just did what had to be done."

Millie looked around in fascination. The room was full of curiosities and wonders, from strange creatures to mechanical devices.

"Welcome to my museum," Mr. MacDonnell said, then added with a wink, "Though the stagecoach company thinks of it as a way station, I prefer to think of it as an oasis for the mind."

"It's their stomachs that need food, Mac," his wife said. "Now let them come and eat, won't you?"

"Don't touch that!" Jedidiah said. Millie turned to see Jaz with a metal tube in her hand.

"Now, now," Mr. MacDonnell said, patting the little girl's head. "I wouldn't have put it out if I didn't want people looking at it! It's a kaleidoscope," he explained, squatting down. "A chap I went to school with invented it. David Brewster. His family intended him for the ministry, but he was always fascinated with bits of glass. Mirrors and lenses, for the most part." He demonstrated how to hold the tube up to the light and peer in the hole at one end. "You turn the tube so . . . " Jaz gasped with delight and held it up for Millie. Bits of colored glass were reflected in two mirrors, producing a pattern like a multicolored snowflake.

"It's beautiful!" Millie said. "Look, Pappa!"

"Too bad the young man did not continue in the ministry," Mrs. Lyone said. "I don't know that making toys is any way to spend a life."

"David was not a brilliant speaker. His sermons would soon have been forgotten. But his toys have given enjoyment to many, many people," Mr. MacDonnell said with a smile. "I like to think that a hundred years from now, a child will see his snowflakes and laugh. Now, I hope I love Jesus as much as any preacher. But my personality tends toward adventures and oddities, and that's the way I can serve Him best. I think He is delighted with my little museum here. It makes people happy."

Millie smiled, thinking of Aunt Wealthy. She tended toward adventure too, and would understand Mr. MacDonnell completely.

"You're going to let them starve to death, are you?" Mrs. MacDonnell had her hands on her hips. "They are hungry people, Mac!"

Mr. MacDonnell beamed. "She delights in pots, pans, recipes, and the like. When she gets to heaven, I think God might let her cook. It'll be as good as anything they serve up there, I'm sure."

Mrs. Lyone looked mildly scandalized. "I don't know about that—" she began, but Stuart offered his arm.

"May I escort you to dinner?" he asked.

"Why, of course," she said, taking his arm, and they followed Mrs. MacDonnell into a handsome dining room, complete with tables covered with cloths and china. "Was that Fenris Jones I saw driving?" Mrs. MacDonnell asked after grace was said. "I thought he was dead."

"I wouldn't mention that to him," Stuart said. "It seems to be a sore point."

"I tried to convince the man to sit with us," Mr. MacDonnell said. "But he wouldn't set foot in the door."

The meal had just begun when the stagecoach horn blew. "What can he be thinking?" Mrs. MacDonnell cried. "You've just settled in!"

Gavi stood up and looked at his brother and sister. "Let's go!"

"I'm hungry, Gavi," Jedidiah said pleadingly. "Can't we just let him go on without us?"

"You know we can't," Gavi said.

Millie looked from the food to the children. "May I?" she asked, indicating a pie. "I will send the tin back on the next stagecoach."

"Help yourself," Mrs. MacDonnell said, "to all you can carry!"

"Excellent idea, daughter!" Stuart said. "Do you have a basket for this chicken?"

"That I do," Mary said. "I'll bring it along. You just delay the driver for me."

Hot cross buns, cheese, radishes, and boiled eggs vanished into pockets, and the travelers hurried out the door. The MacDonnells followed them outside before they reached the stagecoach.

Mr. Jones surveyed them with disgust as they started to board. "That food better not get all over my upholstery," he said.

"We will do our best to be neat." Stuart smiled at him.

"They will try to be neat," Mr. MacDonnell repeated. "Care for a leg?" He held the basket of chicken up toward Fenris Jones.

"Is that some kinda comment?" Fenris Jones demanded.

"Of course not," Mr. MacDonnell said. "It's an offer of dinner."

"I done et already," Fenris said. Millie wondered what he had found to devour in the barn and shook her head at the vision of helpless mice scurrying for cover.

Once inside, Millie looked around in dismay. A picnic without plates, silverware, or napkins in a moving stagecoach was a little more than she had anticipated. "Can we use your newspaper?" Millie asked her father.

Stuart nodded and began to tear and distribute the pages. Soon each traveler had a piece of newspaper. Bread and chicken and cheese had never tasted so good. Those lucky enough to have clean handkerchiefs used them as napkins; the others happily licked their fingers.

Mrs. Lyone declined the pie, but a wonderful mess was had by the rest. Cleanup was attempted using handkerchiefs and leftover newsprint, and then the travelers went back to watching the scenery, much more content and friendly than they had been up to that point.

They had traveled for perhaps an hour and Jaz had snuggled against Jedidiah for a nap, when the stagecoach crested the last hill. Millie had a glimpse of the country spread out before her—a counterpane of fields and forests in shades of green. "Look, how beaut—" she began, and in the next instant let out a gasp, for the road dropped steeply down the other side and the stagecoach gained speed at an astonishing pace. Fenris Jones was shouting at the team for even greater speed.

"We're all going to die!" Mrs. Lyone screamed. Jaz woke from her nap and started to cry, and the stagecoach bounced from side to side, everyone reaching out to steady themselves.

"Focus on the scenery," Millie suggested, holding on to her hat with one hand and her father's arm with the other. "Isn't it lovely?"

"I can't look," Mrs. Lyone wailed. "Is it . . . is it far to the valley floor? No, don't tell me. I don't know that I could bear it!" She clasped her plump hands over her bosom. "Pray with me, Alexander!" she commanded. Alexander folded his hands. "Our Father, who art in—eeeekk!" The right front wheel hit a stone, and the stagecoach careened crazily. "Oh! I don't think I can bear this!"

"We are pulled by six good horses," Stuart assured her. "And God has made them very sensible creatures, even if our driver is not. It would take a great deal of effort to force them over the edge. I'm not sure even Fenris Jones could do it."

"How far is it to the bottom?" Mrs. Lyone asked again.

"Not more than two hundred feet," Millie answered, leaning out the window to check the distance.

Millie's Steadfast Love

"What if a wheel broke?" Jedidiah asked. "What would happen then?"

"We would be catapulted into space," Mrs. Lyone declared. "To certain death!"

During the first steep descent Gavi had pulled his baby sister up onto his lap, apparently fearful that Alexander would land on the child after bouncing into the air. When they slowed briefly, the sound of the whip and Fenris's horrible voice could be heard, cursing the horses and making inarticulate sounds of rage. Millie braced herself as they plunged again. This went on for half an hour, the poor horses first straining up the hills, and then racing down the other side. Each descent seemed longer than the previous one.

At last the shouting ceased. *Have we reached level ground at last?* Millie wondered, glancing at the window. Something was hanging down in front of her. She blinked. Fenris Jones's hand was not on the reins where it should be. It was swaying back and forth just outside her window. *Could the man have lapsed into a drunken stupor?*

"Mr. Jones?" Millie reached out to touch the hand, and just as she did, Mr. Jones's face appeared, upside down and staring at her with wide-open eyes. Millie blinked, and he was gone—tossed over the side. Mrs. Lyone's piercing scream was evidence enough that Millie wasn't seeing things. The road dipped again, and the horses, not waiting for the whip, began to run. Mrs. Lyone screamed again and threw herself on Stuart. "Save us, Mr. Keith!"

"I would be happy to try," Stuart said, trying to unlock her arms from his neck, "if you would free me." Mrs. Lyone just screamed even louder and held on even tighter.

Someone had to stop the stagecoach. Stuart was struggling to free himself from Mrs. Lyone, who appeared to have fainted on top of him. Millie pushed the door open and stood up, gripping the rail at the top with both hands. *Pappa was going to climb up this way*, Millie thought with determination. *Of course we were crawling uphill then, not plunging downhill out of control!* Glancing back, she saw that Gavi had the same idea. He was climbing out the window on the opposite side. The stagecoach bounced, and Millie's cap flew off, tumbling down, down, down into the canyon. Millie tore her eyes away from the empty space, only to see a sheer rock wall closing in on the opposite side of the road. If Gavi was not already on top, he was sure to be crushed, or knocked off and plummeted to a sure death.

"Look out!" Millie called, hoping he could hear. And then the rocks were past. Millie scrambled with her boots against the side of the coach. They caught on her lace pantalets and she very nearly lost her grip before she got the toe of one boot on the front window and pushed up with all her might, catching the back of the driver's seat. From there it was a mad scramble over the top.

Gavi came over the other side, and they reached the seat box almost at the same instant. All six sets of reins were knotted together and looped over the side rail of the seat. "Must have known that he was going," Gavi called out in a high voice, pulling at the knot. He laced three sets of reins through the fingers of each hand.

"Take the brake," he said, "but go easy. The horses are afraid. They're not responding." Millie reached with her foot for the brake lever, then hesitated. Fenris Jones's peg leg was still strapped in place, bouncing crazily as if it were trying to stop the stagecoach all by itself. Millie grimaced as she put her boot on the lever beneath the wooden device.

Millie's Steadfast Love

"Now what?" she asked, looking over at Gavi. He had lost his cap, and a thick braid tumbled over his . . . *her* shoulder.

"Go easy," Gavi said again. *She* let go a piercing whistle with her lips, at the same time pulling back on the reins. The horses' ears came back and they slowed, but not enough. Millie glanced ahead and wished that she hadn't. The road made a hard turn to the left, with nothing to the right but blue sky and canyon. Each pair had to make the turn at just the right moment.

"Gavi . . . " Millie said, trying to keep the fear from her voice, "I think we'd better do something *now*."

"I'm doing it just as fast as I can," Gavi said. "I need leverage!" She stood up just as the right front wheel hit a rut.

"Hold on!" Millie yelled, grabbing Gavi's shirttail with one hand and the rail with the other. The rear wheel hit the rut, bouncing Gavi into the air. Millie pulled her back by her shirttail, and wrapped her arms around her waist to hold her down.

Gavi set her feet, and then the lead horses were at the turn. The leaders made the turn, then the swings, and finally the wheelers, and then the stagecoach itself was flying around the bend, rear wheels skidding on the hard-packed road, coming dangerously close to the cliff's edge. The road straightened again and Gavi whistled, hauling back on the reins. Millie let go of Gavi and applied herself to the brake, and this time the team slowed.

"Thank goodness!" Gavi said, as the road took an upward incline. "Give it some more brake." Millie pushed harder on the lever, bracing her feet and pushing with all her might.

"Whoa!" Gavi called to the team. "Easy now, you're all right." In a matter of moments the stagecoach had come to a complete stop. The door flew open, and Stuart was the first one out.

"Millie Keith!" he said. "Don't you ever scare me like that again! You should have waited for me to go up . . . " He grabbed her in a hug that nearly squeezed her breath out. "Never mind. I'm proud of you. A man simply doesn't expect to be saved by his daughter."

Mrs. Lyone and Alexander tumbled out, leaning shakily on each other, and Jedidiah followed with Jaz in his arms.

"Thank you, young man—" Mrs. Lyone's jaw dropped open. She was staring up at Gavi's braid. "You could not possibly be a girl," she said. "I don't know . . . "

"You don't know much, do you?" Jed said.

"Jedidiah Paul Mikolaus," Gavi said sternly. "You will not speak to your elders that way! What would Mamma think?"

"That's right!" Mrs. Lyone said. "I was just saying that a girl could not possibly have stopped a runaway coach."

"Ma," Alexander interrupted. Everyone looked at him. "She's a girl too," he said, pointing at Millie.

"That is not the point!" Mrs. Lyone said, stamping her foot. "*She* was a girl when she crawled out the window—not a young man one moment and a young lady the next. It's unsettling, and I was already quite unsettled."

"We will have to go back for the driver," Stuart said. "I have never handled a six-horse team, but—"

"I have," Gavi said, looking slightly offended. "Unless any of you had a problem with my driving just now, I think I am best suited to continue."

Stuart looked flustered for a moment. "Yes, of course. You handled the team very well."

"Good," Gavi said. "When the road is wider, we will turn around. Will everyone get back inside now?"

Stuart nodded, but Mrs. Lyone folded her arms. "You cannot be serious, Mr. Keith! Letting this child drive this group of runaway horses!" said Mrs. Lyone indignantly.

"She just saved your life," Millie pointed out. "Doesn't that make a difference?"

"It does seem the best solution, Mrs. Lyone," Stuart said. "I don't know how to handle a team of six."

"Do you want to ride up here with me?" Gavi asked Millie.

"Of course," Millie said. "That is, if Pappa doesn't mind."

"I could use someone on the brake," said Gavi. "There are some hills between here and there."

Stuart agreed, and helped Millie back up into the seat box. Gavi, in her boy's pants, had a much easier time climbing up.

"I want to ride with you, Gavi," Jedidiah said. "I can help."

"I know you could," his sister said. "But I need you to take care of Jaz for me."

Millie set about the unpleasant task of freeing Fenris Jones's peg leg from the brake lever. She handed it down to her father.

"What are you going to do with that?" Alexander asked.

"Put it in the luggage box," Stuart said. "Perhaps Mr. Jones will still need it when we find him." Gavi studied him a moment before agreeing.

"I don't see why we have to look for him," Mrs. Lyone said. "I think we should leave him where he is."

"Surely you don't mean that," Millie said. "It might be days before someone travels this road and finds him. He could be suffering."

"We have suffered enough under his dictatorship," Mrs. Lyone sniffed. "A little taste of his own medicine might be good for his soul!"

The passengers climbed aboard once again. Gavi called out to the team, let out a slight whistle, and they started out. "How did you learn to drive a team?" Millie asked.

"My family are horse traders and tinkers," Gavi explained. "If it's horses or mending things, we know how to do it. We've traded horses from the coast to the Indian nations."

"Are you going to meet your parents?" Millie asked.

Gavi was silent for a moment. "We are on our way to Lansdale, Ohio," she said.

"Really? I know almost everyone in Lansdale. I grew up there!"

Gavi's black eyes flashed at her. "Do you know a woman named Stanhope? Miss Wealthy Stanhope?"

CHAPTER

A New Look

There is a time for everything,
and a season for every
activity under heaven.

ECCLESIASTES 3:1

A New Look

"*W*ealthy Stanhope!" Millie exclaimed, almost falling over the side.

Gavi gave her a sideways look. "You know her?"

"She's my aunt! We are on our way to visit her before we go home to Indiana. How do *you* know her?"

"I've never met her. She was once my grandmother's best friend," Gavi said. "They met in Philadelphia when they were both girls and stayed close over the years through correspondence. Gran always said . . . " Her voice trailed off.

"Your parents have sent you to visit then?"

"I think I can turn the team here," said Gavi. The road had dropped into a valley of wide meadows and trees. "It's a risk, but I don't think we'll find a better spot before the next station."

Millie studied Gavi as the girl concentrated on controlling the team and making the turnaround. There was something very sad about the set of her mouth, something sad and haunting about the look in her eyes. *They are in trouble,* Millie thought. Millie gripped the rail as they lurched crazily, and then they were on the road again, heading back the way they had come.

"What's she like?" Gavi asked. "Miss Stanhope, I mean."

Millie smiled. "She is indescribable, really. She has a great faith in Jesus, and she's been following Him all of her life."

"Sounds like Gran," Gavi said. "She had the greatest faith of any person I have ever met."

"Had?"

"She's been gone for six months." Gavi's voice was tight with emotion. She gave Millie a measuring look. "You believe in Jesus, then?"

"Yes," Millie said, "with all my heart."

"Were you afraid—when you were climbing on top of the stagecoach? Or did you believe that Jesus would keep you from falling?" asked Gavi. Her eyes were on the horses, but every line of her body was tense, waiting for Millie's answer.

"I do believe God has good plans for me," Millie said carefully. "And that is very easy to say, sitting here right now. But while I was hanging on the side and the canyon dropped off beneath me . . . I was terrified! But I wasn't really thinking about what might happen to me. I was thinking about what would happen to everyone if I didn't act. Weren't you afraid?"

"Yes," Gavi said simply, "but I have to take care of my brother and sister. I wouldn't have believed you if you had not been afraid. Or if you had said you were not."

They rode in silence for a time. "Do you believe the Bible is true in the same way for everyone?" Gavi finally asked.

"I'm not sure I understand the question." Millie had the uncomfortable feeling that the test wasn't over, that every word she said was important. *Lord, help me choose the right words,* she silently prayed.

"Do you know the verse, '"For I know the plans I have for you," declares the Lord, "plans to prosper you and not to harm you, plans to give you hope and a future"'?" Gavi asked.

"Yes," Millie said. "That's Jeremiah 29:11."

"Do you think that is true for everyone?" Gavi asked doubtfully.

Charles Landreth, Millie thought suddenly. She prayed every day for Charles to have hope and a future, for Charles to find Jesus. *I can't love someone more than Jesus does,* Millie reminded herself.

"Yes I do," said Millie. "When you love someone, you want what's best for them. God loves each one of us like that."

Gavi was silent again as the horses made their way back up the steep road. Millie prayed silently for the girl, unsure what to say or do. "I want you to know something, Gavi," she said at last. "You can trust Wealthy Stanhope with anything. Anything at all."

Gavi's eyes closed for a moment as if she were praying, and when she opened them again, tears sparkled on her lashes. She wiped them away almost savagely.

"How did you learn to drive a stagecoach?" Millie asked, searching for a less painful subject.

"My mother taught me," Gavi said, with a weak smile. "We traded horses, raised and trained them too, for saddle and for pulling wagons and coaches."

"Your mother?" Millie said in surprise. "I would think your father would have been the horse trainer."

"And girls can't stop runaway coaches," Gavi said with a laugh.

"I see your point." Millie smiled back at her.

"The gift runs in my mother's family," Gavi said. "It came with Gran from the old country — from Spain."

"You are Spanish, then?"

"We are Romani." She glanced at Millie as she pulled the reins to the right. "A thousand generations ago my people left India. We have no home anymore. I've heard it said that Romani make people glad twice — once when we come to do the work they do not want to do and again when we leave."

"Romani people don't settle down?"

"Some do," Gavi shrugged. "Some of us have homes where we live and die, just like other people. But others

have the wander in them. My mother had the wander. Father followed her because he loved her. The road was our home."

Millie tried to imagine what it would be like to have no place to call her own. *As much as I like adventures, I like to think of my family waiting at home. And my friends. It takes only a moment to make a new friend, but years to grow a friendship. I wonder if Gavi and Jed and Jaz have any friends? Do they have anyone waiting for them anywhere?*

"Oh, it's not so bad," Gavi said, seeing the look on Millie's face. "At least it wasn't for Mamma and me. We had the horses, you see. We understand them and they understand us. That's our gift. Gran had it. Jaz has it, too. Give her a moment with a horse and it will be following her like a puppy. But Jedidiah's like Father. He's better with wheels than with horses."

"Do the horses really understand what you say?"

This time Gavi laughed. "Gran always said that the gift was simply understanding what God made horses to be. Perhaps God gives the gift to the horses, instead of to us. They simply understand what we need them to do. They understand that we love them." The more Gavi talked, the more she relaxed.

She's really a very beautiful girl when she doesn't have her cap pulled down and a cold, hard look on her face, thought Millie.

"A well-trained team is worth quite a lot, you know. These," said Gavi, indicating the team that was pulling the stagecoach, "See how well-matched they are in shade and height? They move together well, too. The near leader is a little slow to respond, but they are a good team. They'll make their fifteen miles a day in good time. They would bring a trader six hundred dollars as they are. But Jehus want more than that. They want a team that can put on a show coming into the station. If you gave me these boys for a few weeks, I could sell them for eight hundred, at least. They just need a little polish. We could teach them to dance into the station and bow to the ladies once they got there."

"What's a Jay-hoo?" Millie asked. "George, the other driver, used that word too."

"A crack driver," Gavi explained. "Like Jehu in the Bible, who drove fast and furious. They all *think* they're Jehus."

"You could teach these horses to dance?"

Gavi considered them. "It would take me three months," she said at last. "Maybe four. If we could stay anywhere that long."

"Gavi," Millie said. "I . . . I don't mean to pry—"

"Then don't." Gavi's smile disappeared and she turned her face away.

"I don't know what kind of trouble you're in," Millie continued, "but it's clear you are in some kind of difficulty. My Pappa is a good lawyer, and he's a very smart man. And if you are friends of Aunt Wealthy, I know she would recommend him. Lawyers keep their client's business strictly confidential. I want you to know that. Pappa wouldn't even tell me."

Gavi remained silent, and Millie was sure she had made a mistake. *Lord, what have I done? I wanted to help Gavi, but now I am afraid I've ruined her willingness to speak to me. You know what's wrong. Please use me to help her.*

They drove on without a word between them until they spotted the crumpled form of the driver lying in the middle of the road.

"Doesn't seem like Mrs. Lyone's medicine's going to do him much good," Gavi said, pulling the horses up. "At least not from here."

Stuart was the first one to reach the still form. He knelt bedside the lifeless body and gently closed the dead man's eyes. "Apoplexy," he said, taking one of the dead man's arms. "He was dead before he hit the road. Would you mind helping me, Alexander?" Alexander took the other arm and they started to drag Fenris Jones toward the coach. The horses snorted and stomped at the scent of the man.

"Horsie, horsie!" Jaz called, clapping her hands. The near leader, the one Gavi had said was slow to respond to the reins, dropped his head and drew in a great breath, then blew it out through his lips. Jaz laughed and reached up for him.

"Jedidiah, mind your sister," Gavi called.

"What are you doing?" Mrs. Lyone had finally disembarked. "He's not riding in *this* stagecoach!"

"We can't leave him here for the animals," Millie said.

"Therefore," Stuart dropped Fenris Jones's hand, straightened his back, and grimaced, "he must come with us."

"I'm sure that's not necessary," Mrs. Lyone argued. "They will send someone along for the horrible man. Alexander, put him down this instant." She planted herself between Stuart Keith and the stagecoach.

Alexander suddenly realized that he was still holding the dead man's hand. He dropped it and rubbed his palms on his pants.

"Mr. Jones wasn't *completely* horrible," Millie pointed out. "He saved our lives."

"He did?" asked Jedidiah, who had dragged Jaz away from the horses, apparently finding a dead man much more interesting.

Gavi nodded. "The last thing he did was to tie off the reins. If he hadn't done that, the lines would have tangled. We'd have gone over the cliff."

"Well . . . if we must take him, we must," Mrs. Lyone sniffed. "I'm going to take a short walk while you settle this as you see fit, Mr. Keith."

"Would you mind taking the children with you?" Stuart asked. "I don't think they need to be here."

"Gavi—" Jedidiah began, but his older sister shushed him.

"You go on with Mrs. Lyone," she said. The boy kicked the wheel on his way past, but he went.

"Where's he going to ride, Pappa?" Millie asked, looking from the huge, still form to the bulging leather sack on the back of the seat. She had seen weary travelers crawl into an empty boot for a nap, but this one was not empty. It was completely filled with mail bags. "His peg leg barely fit in, Pappa. I'm sure the rest of him won't."

"We could sit him up in the seat," Gavi suggested. "He could take Millie's place."

"I don't think I could ride with a dead man," Alexander said. "I just don't think I could."

"We will have to fasten him on top," Stuart said. Gavi and Alexander climbed to the top, ready to grab the body and pull it up, as Millie and her father tried to lift him. As in life, Fenris Jones did not seem to want to cooperate; his limp weight was too heavy, even for the two of them together. Millie changed places with Alexander, but they had no more success with this arrangement. "I'm open to suggestions," Stuart said at last.

"If we had a rope . . ." Alexander began.

"If wishes were horses," Gavi said with a shrug. "We have no rope."

"Could he ride on top of the boot?" Millie asked, pushing a stray strand of hair from her eyes. "Can we lift him that high?" Mr. Jones's body was lifted again, this time to the top of the boot. They had to settle him in a sitting position, and Gavi and Alexander donated their suspenders to strap him in place.

"I hope you are not planning on turning around again?" Mrs. Lyone said as Stuart helped her in. "It was quite bumpy last time."

"The horses have gone their distance," Gavi said. "We must be five or six miles from the station now, and they've come farther than that already. They won't make it to the next station. We have to go back." She didn't sound as if she would take any argument. "Jedidiah? Would you like to ride in the box with me? That is, if Millie would watch Jaz."

"Of course," Millie said, but she was certain Gavi was trying to get rid of her.

Millie settled herself in the seat alongside her father and pulled Jaz onto her lap. The distance to the station seemed to have doubled, in no small part because of the unpleasant thumping of Fenris Jones's head against the back of the coach every time they went over a bump. Each time it happened, Alexander jumped and Mrs. Lyone gasped.

"Dead men can't hurt you," Jaz informed them the first time it happened. "Don't be scared."

Are you afraid of someone? Millie longed to ask. *Is there someone who can hurt you?* Millie bit her tongue and pulled out the length of yarn for another game of cat's cradle.

When they pulled into MacDonnell's way station at last, another stagecoach had just arrived in the yard. A crowd gathered around as Stuart handed Gavi down from the box with calls of "What's wrong? Why are you back?"

"A girl!" the driver of the second stagecoach said. "A girl was driving!"

"You sure?" asked a young man who was apparently his son. Gavi ignored them.

"Gentlemen," Stuart said, "I suggest you direct your energy to something more productive, such as helping me with Fenris Jones." The whole crowed followed him around to the boot.

"Well, I'll be darned." The young man pushed his hat back. "Fenris Jones. I thought he was dead!"

"Watch how you talk!" the driver said, smacking him on the back of his head. "He *is* dead!" This having been firmly established by everyone in the group and formally announced by Mr. MacDonnell, it was determined that the body would be buried behind the station and information sent to any living relatives.

"I have pine slats left over from siding the barn," the hostler said. "I can make him a box." Mr. MacDonnell himself took one shovel and Stuart Keith another, and the two men set out to dig a grave. The ladies were ushered inside while the men took the body to the barn.

"Now what's this all about?" asked Mrs. MacDonnell, looking Gavi up and down. "A snip of a thing like you, driving a coach and six!" She broke into a smile. "That will show those Jehus what's what — parading around as if they were God's gift! You'll be famous, you know. Everyone along the line will hear about it."

"I'm afraid so," Gavi said. "Do you mind if I use a room to change?"

"I certainly don't mind," said the woman. As Gavi retrieved a bag, Mrs. MacDonnell asked Millie, "Would you like to straighten up too?"

Millie glanced at her reflection in the glass front of a china cabinet and her hand flew to her hair. "Yes, thank you," she said, blushing. She'd had no idea she was in such disarray, and it occurred to her for the first time that her periwinkle cap was gone forever.

They followed Mrs. MacDonnell to a room at the back of the house where the kind woman provided a pitcher of water, soap, towels, and bowl.

"I don't really like wearing pants," Gavi said, as she pulled a skirt, blouse, and petticoats from her bag. "But they're useful when you're working with horses."

Millie washed her face and hands and combed out her hair, twisting it into a bun and pinning it in place while Gavi dressed.

"That's better," Gavi sighed, surveying herself in the mirror. "I feel more like myself." Her maroon-red blouse brought out the roses in her lips and cheeks. As Gavi wound her long braid around her head to form a crown, Millie wondered how she had ever mistaken Gavi for a boy, or thought she was fifteen for that matter. *Gavi is clearly nineteen or twenty — older than I am. It's her slight build that made her appear so young.*

"Yay!" Jaz said, clapping her hands. "Gavriel's back!"

"Why on earth were you wearing boys' clothes?" Mrs. Lyone asked. "Was it some kind of disguise?"

Gavi started to reply, but at that moment the men came in, apparently having done all they could for Mr. Jones.

"Pa," the young man said, elbowing the driver and pointing at Gavi. "Pa, look . . . "

The driver shook his head. "That's a girl, all right. I said it before. Now shut your mouth, boy, before a fly gets in."

"You young ladies come with me," Mrs. MacDonnell said, frowning at the men. Mrs. Lyone started to follow them, but when Mrs. MacDonnell added, "I need some help in the kitchen," she settled back into her chair.

A New Look

"The truth is," Mrs. MacDonnell said when the door was closed, "I would dearly like to hear the tale, so I will brew you some tea if you sit and talk. Supper will be a little late, as there are extra mouths to feed."

"May I help you with the cooking?" Millie offered. "I have often helped my mother in the kitchen."

"I would offer to help," Gavi said with a shrug, "but I'm not much use in the kitchen."

"You leave it to us, then, dear girl," Mrs. MacDonnell said as Millie strapped on an apron. "My poor guests have had quite enough excitement for one day. They don't need any surprises on their plates."

Mrs. MacDonnell made clucking and tsking noises with her tongue as Gavi and Millie relayed the events of the day, and when the story was done she put her hands on her hips and looked at the girls. "What would your mothers think?" She shook her head and winked. "I'm thinking they would be very proud."

A course of action for the travelers was decided at the supper table. First thing in the morning, they would take the larger of the two coaches, which seated nine, and everyone would travel on to the next station. The men and extra mailbags would ride on top. Fenris Jones's coach would be left for the stage company to send for at a later date.

Fenris himself was buried behind the station after their meal was done. Six men carried the pine box up the hill, followed by Mrs. MacDonnell and the women. Stuart brought his Bible along and read a few lines from the fourteenth chapter of the book of John and the twenty-first chapter of the book of Revelation. Mr. MacDonnell offered a prayer and then looked around at the small crowd. "Fenris told me once that no one would attend his

Millie's Steadfast Love

funeral if he died," he said. "And look at us! Weeping and all."

"I always cry at funerals," Mrs. Lyone said defensively.

One by one, they all turned and left the grave. Stuart tucked Millie's hand under his arm as they started back. They stood by the corral as Mr. MacDonnell and the hostler transferred their trunks and the mail to the larger stage. It was the first chance Millie had to speak to her Pappa alone since they arrived. He had a faraway, thoughtful look on his face. *Is he thinking about poor Mr. Jones? Or Gavi's trouble?*

"A penny for your thoughts, Pappa," Millie said. "It's my turn now."

"Do you remember what your Uncle Horace said about traveling with you?" he asked.

"About my being a menace?"

Stuart nodded. "I think he may have been on to something."

"Pappa!"

"Oh, all right," he said. "I was thinking about the Mikolaus children."

"Pappa! They are going to Aunt Wealthy's!"

"*Our* Aunt Wealthy?"

"None other," said Millie. Then she described the conversation she'd had with Gavi. "I spoke too hastily, Pappa," she confessed. "I should have given her more time. Gavi was starting to talk to me, but . . . I just don't think it went well. Perhaps I shouldn't have spoken, or perhaps I should have used different words. I should have done *something* differently. I made a muddle of the whole thing."

"Don't be too hard on yourself," Stuart said. "You were trying to do the right thing. If Jesus can use even our mistakes,

60

how much more can He use us when we are trying to help? If He wants you to help, He will give you another chance." He smiled and added, "And if they're going to our very own Aunt Wealthy's, I'm sure God has a plan."

CHAPTER

Grave Concerns

Surely he will save you from
the fowler's snare and from
the deadly pestilence.

PSALM 91:3

Grave Concerns

*M*illie shut her new Bible and set it on the table in front of her. She'd given her old one to Charles on the day she turned down his proposal. Stuart had been very pleased with this new Bible, showing her the concordance included in the back. "Mine is so convenient," he'd said. "I can't always remember just the verse I need. Sometimes I don't even know the verse. But if I can think of one word in the verse and look for that, well, I can find the Scripture."

Her father may have been pleased, but Millie was not. She'd been able to turn to almost any verse of any book in her old Bible without looking. The pages of this new Bible were stiff, and because of the added bulk, nothing seemed to be in the right place. The only book it opened to easily was First Corinthians because Millie spent so much time there. *Has Charles read 1 Corinthians 13? Love is patient, but I am not. I want to know that Charles is reading the Bible. I want to know if he ever thinks about me the way I think about him.* She rested her forehead on the Bible. *Why, why, why can't God just tell me what is happening with Charles?* She realized that she was banging her head on the Bible in rhythm with her whys, and looked around quickly. Stuart was reading a new newspaper in the corner and hadn't noticed, but a stylish woman at the next table frowned at her over her tea. Millie sighed and opened the Bible again. *God, please help me to be patient . . .*

An unexpected layover while a wheel was repaired had given Millie more time to think and pray than she'd had since leaving Philadelphia. Mrs. Lyone and Alexander had said their good-byes two days after Fenris died, and Millie

Millie's Steadfast Love

was still trying to become accustomed to the quiet. Jaz was fascinated by Millie's hats and fashionable dresses, and liked to sit with her right beside her, but Gavi had kept so much to herself since they left MacDonnell station that Millie was surprised to look up and find the girl smiling at her.

"Why such a solemn face, Millie Keith?"

"I . . . It's complicated," Millie said.

Gavriel nodded. "I'm going to take Jaz window-shopping. Would you like to come with us? Unless you would prefer to pound the Bible with your head."

"Oh, you saw that?" Millie asked sheepishly. Gavriel nodded, but said nothing more. "I would like a walk," Millie said, truly grateful for the offer. "Just let me put my Bible away."

She stopped to speak to her father on the way out of the room. "A stroll sounds marvelous," he said, smiling. "Don't let me hold you up, but I believe I might follow when I finish this."

Millie took a moment to gather a feathered hat that always cheered her and her parasol. Heat waves shimmered off the cobblestones of the street when they stepped outside.

"Is Jedidiah coming with us?" Millie asked as she opened her parasol. It may have been fashionable, petite, and lacy, but she couldn't help thinking that Aunt Wealthy's purple umbrella provided more shade.

"Jed's long gone," Gavi said. "He earned a nickel chopping wood and has gone to spend it."

"Can I please?" Jaz asked, pointing at the parasol. Millie let the little girl take it, and she walked ahead of them, twirling it over her shoulder.

They stopped at each and every window, while Jaz exclaimed in delight over each new item she saw, until they came to Honest Lloyd's Mercantile, which had a piano on display in the window.

"What's that?" the little girl asked.

"A piano," Millie informed her. "It makes music." Jaz pressed her ear against the window, looked up at Millie, and shook her head.

"It doesn't make music all by itself," Millie said, laughing. "It needs help."

"Can you help it?"

"I can try," Millie said. She led the way into the shop and stopped to look at the piano. It wasn't fancy or expensive like the one she had played at Roselands. It was very plain, in fact. The kind of piano you might find in a small church or in the parlor of a working family. She picked up the sheet music that lay on top of the case.

"I see you are interested in music." Millie was so intent on the notes that she jumped at the sound of the shop-keeper's voice.

"Arthur Lloyd, at your service, ladies." He offered a bow. "Would you like to try the piano?"

Millie glanced around the mercantile. There were several customers, all intent on their own business. "If you wouldn't mind."

"Of course not, of course not." The man had an unfortunate habit of wringing his hands. He paused in the wringing long enough to pull the bench out for Millie. She seated herself and looked at the keys. When she left Roselands she hadn't wanted to play again, at least not for a long, long time. She had spent so much time at the piano there, believing she was purchasing freedom for Laylie. She had worked so hard at learning new pieces. So much time wasted. She had never wanted to play the piano again, she was sure.

Now, even though it had only been a few weeks, her fingers positively itched for the feel of keys.

"Here you are," said Mr. Lloyd as he placed a sheet of music in front of her.

"Thank you," Millie said, but she closed her eyes. The only sheet music she needed was in her mind. She touched the keys and the music flowed—sometimes soft and gentle, like prayers whispered to God, and other times intense and loud, as if she were shouting the emotions of her heart to God. Finally, laughing that the piano sounded so good, Millie let her hands fall from the keys.

Someone was clapping. She opened her eyes and saw to her embarrassment that the customers had gathered around. Jaz was clapping wildly. "Music!" she yelled. "Music, music, music!"

"Indeed, young lady, that was music!" Mr. Lloyd was wringing his hands furiously. "I think you have found your instrument. I can give this model to you for just one hundred and twenty dollars, shipping included!"

"I'm sorry," Millie said. "I don't have any money."

"Could my Clarabelle learn to play like that?" a woman demanded. "I might buy it." Mr. Lloyd turned to her, and Millie slipped off of the piano seat. She ushered Jaz and Gavi out the door.

Gavi was looking at her seriously. "Clarabelle is not going to be able to do what you just did, Millie Keith," she said. "You have a gift too," said Gavi. "Not horses—pianos. Or maybe it's just the music. I could tell when you were playing."

"Maybe," Millie said. "But it seems to me that raising horses is more profitable. My piano playing has brought me nothing but trouble."

Gavi gave her a strange look. "Maybe that's the way it is with gifts," Gavi said. "People are going to want what you have. They are going to want to use it, try to make it their own."

Like Aunt Isabel used me to entertain her guests, Millie thought. *She wanted music and laughter, and she had none of her own.* "Don't you think God gives everyone something special that they can do?"

"I don't know," Gavriel said. "I think maybe . . . " She stopped in mid-sentence. "Tell me that's not Jed!" They followed the sound of his voice down an alley and onto another street. He had stacked shipping crates together to make a stage in the shade of an oak tree, and already a small crowd had gathered.

"Hurry, hurry, step right up! You don't need newspapers, folks. Why wait for the ink to dry? Get the news from an eyewitness! Spend a nickel to hear the most exciting story in the state—the Daring Maidens and the Dead Man's Ride!" He held his cap out, and people threw in nickels and pennies. He snatched them neatly from the air and put them in his pocket. "Twenty more cents, just twenty more cents! Hear a story that will chill your bones and set your knees to quaking. You will never ride a stagecoach again . . . "

"Daring Maidens? I'm going to kill him," Gavi said matter-of-factly. "Will you watch Jaz for me?" She started to push her way through the crowd, but a man in a striped suit tossed a coin that looked like a silver dollar.

"Here, you rascal," he called. "Let's hear that story!"

"Fair enough," Jed said, holding up the coin. "I'll tell you . . . "

A woman barred Gavriel's way. "None of that, now," she said. "No shoving. I paid my nickel, and I want to hear!"

"Fenris Jones was a stagecoach driver," Jed called out. "On the very line that runs right through the heart of your town. You might have seen him yourself. A grim-looking fellow with one peg leg."

"That's true," a man called. "I knowed Fenris."

"You don't know him anymore," Jed said. "He's dead, and this is how it happened . . . ."

He proceeded to tell the story, from beginning to end, frequently pausing with great dramatic timing for the highlights. When he reached the point where Gavriel and Millie crawled out the windows of the stagecoach, a man called out, "I want my money back! You said it was a true story!"

"I'm not giving it back," Jed said, "because it is true, just as sure as I'm standing here. I was on that stagecoach, and . . . " The man made an ugly noise and started toward Jed.

"It's true, I tell you! There they are —" He pointed at Millie and Gavi. "Those are the girls that did it!" The crowd turned. Millie felt ridiculous. Doing what had to be done — even if it was stopping a stagecoach — was one thing. Becoming a spectacle was quite another. *Mamma has always said that a lady does not make a spectacle of herself, either by her dress or by her actions.*

"Those girls?" the angry man said. "I want my money back, kid. Those young ladies couldn't stop a runaway stagecoach."

"The kid's tellin' the truth." It was the driver who had brought them from the MacDonnell station. "I helped bury

Fenris Jones, and I saw her," he pointed at Gavi, "drive the stagecoach in with poor ole Fenris strapped to the back like a side of meat."

"I told you," Jed said, but the crowd was paying no attention to him now. They were focused on Millie and Gavriel.

"Would you sit for a picture?" the man in the striped suit asked. "I sell patent medicine, and I would be happy to pay you to endorse my product. Vitalis Extra Life Elixir —" he waved his hand in the air, imagining his poster, "—makes a heroine of you!"

"But we weren't taking Vitalis," Millie pointed out.

"Doesn't matter, doesn't matter one bit. The buying public won't know that. And you could have been, young lady. It wouldn't do you any harm!"

"I don't think so," Stuart Keith stepped up. "I think it is time for my daughter and her friends to return to the station." He picked up Jaz, much to her delight, and carried her as Millie and Gavi followed along. Jedidiah wiggled through the crowd and slipped into step with them.

Gavi grabbed him by his collar. "What do you think you were doing?" she said.

"Making us," he jingled the coins in his pocket, "one dollar and three bits richer. It was a good story, Gavi. The people were happy. And good stories shouldn't just sit around. They have to be told."

"I can't help but think," Stuart said to his daughter later that night, "that it is probably a good thing Jedidiah Mikolaus and Cyril Keith don't know each other." Millie could only nod in agreement.

"Do you think Aunt Wealthy will be able to manage?" she asked.

"I have great confidence in Wealthy," Stuart said with a smile.

"Are they likely to be with her long?" asked Millie.

"I hope so," he said. "I can only hope so."

———— ∿ ————

Millie's anticipation grew as they drew nearer to Lansdale. Not only would she see Aunt Wealthy, but they planned to stay for three days, long enough to catch up with old friends.

When they reached the outskirts of town Millie realized that a lump was forming in her throat. The town had grown, but the farther they went the more familiar the streets and buildings became. This place was part of her, part of her past. Almost every corner held memories of Bea and Camilla and Annabeth, and the fun they'd had together as children. Millie was eager to hear the details of Annabeth's April wedding. She was Mrs. Frank Osborne now. Millie smiled. Lansdale was like the beginning of home, and she had been away from home far too long.

Jedidiah leaned out the window. "Have we ever been here before, Gavi?"

"No," his sister said. "Lots of towns look like this."

They pulled into the downtown station, and the driver called for the passengers to disembark. Millie noted that in the past they had pulled right up to Aunt Wealthy's door.

"Lansdale's grown up," the driver explained. "So many folks travel through we can't drop 'em all off now. Most take a street cab to their destination." He said the last word with relish, as if he were glad the town was large enough to have such things as destinations. "Why, it's got a zoo with a real live lion these days!"

"Let's walk, Pappa," Millie said. "You could go with us, Gavi. It's not far. We can have the trunks sent later."

"It would be good for Jed and Jaz," Gavi agreed. "They have been sitting too long."

Arrangements were made for the trunks and bags, and they started off together.

"What if she's mean, Gavi?" Jed asked. "Do we have to stay?"

"Wait and see," Gavi said, but she was looking more than a little nervous. They turned the corner onto Wealthy's tree-shaded lane.

"There it is," Stuart said, pointing at Wealthy's house. Wealthy Stanhope's garden was an explosion of roses, hollyhocks, daisies, and trumpet vine. Some were planted in an orderly manner, standing as sentinels along the walk, but many more seemed to have volunteered to fill every nook and cranny with color. "What do you think?"

"I don't think they're going to let us in," Jed said.

"Of course she will let you in," Millie said, taking Jaz's hand. "I'm sure she has rooms all prepared for you."

"I don't think so," Gavi's voice was hoarse. "She doesn't know we're coming."

"You didn't write?" asked Millie in surprise.

"There wasn't time," Gavriel blushed. "We would've arrived before the letter. If I'd had any choice . . . "

"I don't mean Miss Stanhope," Jed said. "I mean the copper who's standing in front of the house." Millie had assumed that the man was simply walking his beat, but on closer inspection, she realized Jed was right. He was standing beside Wealthy's gate, and he didn't look like he was going anywhere. A yellow flag fluttered behind him, hanging from Aunt Wealthy's porch.

"Pappa, what does that flag mean?" Millie asked with concern.

"It's a quarantine flag," Stuart said. His brows drew together. "Wealthy must have sickness in her house."

"That's about as far as you go," the policeman said when they reached the gate. "Doctor's orders and the mayor's, too. This is a pox house."

"*Smallpox?*" Millie shuddered. Smallpox killed not only the very young and very old, but people in their prime. Although some escaped a bout with the illness with only a few scars, she had seen the marred faces and blind eyes of smallpox victims. "Pappa, if Aunt Wealthy needs me . . . "

The policeman shook his head. "You don't want to go in there, miss. If you go in, you're not coming out until the sickness is done. They've been at it for three weeks now, and maybe six to go, as someone new keeps coming down with it."

"They?" Stuart asked.

"You know how Miss Stanhope is," the officer shrugged. "Always dragging home beggars and strays." Gavi drew her brother and sister closer as he continued. "A poor family stopped at the church, and their little boy was burning up, so she took them home. They've all got it now, all but the lady who came to help."

"Thank goodness Wealthy has help," Stuart said, just as the door opened.

"Mamma!" Millie cried out in surprise. She tried to step past the guard, but he blocked her way. Marcia Keith looked more than tired. She looked exhausted. Her hair, usually neatly arranged, was falling around her shoulders.

"Marcia, what are you doing here? Are the children with you? Are they ill?" asked Stuart. Millie had never seen fear in her father's eyes before.

"The children are safe in Pleasant Plains," Marcia assured him. "Wealthy wrote that a friend staying at her house had developed the pox. My heart was so heavy when I read the letter that I was sure the Lord was speaking to me. You have no reason to fear for me, Stuart. I was vaccinated as a child. I cannot contract the disease."

"How many invalids do you have?" Stuart asked.

"Six." She leaned against the door frame and Millie was sure it was to keep her knees from buckling.

"Is Wealthy able to help you?" Stuart asked.

"Aunt Wealthy . . . has the pox, Stuart," Marcia said with trepidation.

Millie's hand flew to her mouth. "Who is helping you, Mamma?"

Marcia ignored the question. "I want you all to go home," she said. Millie could tell she was trying to sound cheerful and brave. "I left the children with neighbors. I will be back in Pleasant Plains as soon as possible."

"You're the only one tending them, aren't you?" Stuart took a step toward the guard.

"Stuart, I see what you're thinking," Marcia said. "Don't you dare come in here. Don't you dare! Someone needs to go home and take care of the children. If I had known you would be home soon I would never have left."

"You heard the lady," the guard said. "If you go in there, you can't come back out."

"Let me go, Pappa," Millie said. "I know I can help."

Stuart turned to Millie. "You have never had smallpox or been vaccinated," he said. "I, on the other hand, received vaccination as a student in law school. You go on home and take care of your brothers and sisters. Your mother and I will be along as soon as possible."

As soon as possible. Millie swallowed. *Sickness often follows sickness through a house, with the poor invalids too weak to fight off the next wave of illness.* "Yes, Pappa," Millie said, choking back her tears.

Stuart gathered her in his arms and hugged her tight, then set her on her feet. "Here is enough money to get you home, and tell your brothers I said to obey you until we return. They know what will happen when I get home if they don't."

"Stuart!" Mamma said. "You musn't do this!"

"You can't go in there!" the guard said. "Mayor's orders!"

"Young man," Stuart said, "that lady is my wife. She is all alone tending a houseful of invalids. Now, are you going to get out of my way, or am I going to have to move you?"

The guard's Adam's apple bounced once, and he moved aside. Stuart Keith was up the steps in two bounds. He gathered his wife in his arms.

"What's going to happen to us?" Jed asked. Millie had forgotten all about the Mikolaus sisters and their brother. Jaz and Jed were standing very close to Gavriel. The girl's face was very pale. Millie looked to her father with a hopeful look on her face. He gave the slightest nod and a soft smile.

"You're coming with me," Millie said to Jed. "You are all coming home with me."

CHAPTER

6

A Heavy Heart

"Do not let your hearts be troubled. Trust in God; trust also in me."

JOHN 14:1

A Heavy Heart

tuart! You can't send them on alone!" Marcia exclaimed. "It's not proper, and Millie can't possibly—"

"Marcia," Stuart said firmly, "Millie has taken care of herself in a very difficult situation for almost a year. She has shown great wisdom in her choices. She will be fine on the rest of the journey and I am confident that she can run the house without us for a few weeks."

"But Stuart, it's our job to . . . "

He tipped her chin up. "*My* job right now is taking care of my beautiful bride. That's what Jesus would do. His bride is very special to Him, you know. I think I know how He feels."

Marcia wiped a tear from her face with the palm of her hand and turned to her daughter. "Millie, are you sure you can manage?"

"Yes, Mamma. You just help Aunt Wealthy get well. I will take care of the children. God will help me."

"But how will you . . . where will you spend the night tonight?"

"We'll go to Bea's," Millie said. "You know there is always room at the Hartley house for visitors. How long do you think it will be before you can come home?"

"Six more weeks," the officer said when Stuart didn't answer. "I've been counting, I should know. If nobody else comes down with the pox, they can open the house in six weeks."

Stuart wrapped his arms around his wife again. "We won't be able to write, Millie. Even letters from this house could spread the disease. But I will expect to receive a letter from you at least once a week."

Millie's Steadfast Love

"Yes, Pappa."

"Don't let the boys misbehave," Marcia's voice was firm again. "And make sure Fan keeps after her spelling. And Bobforshort is not to sleep in Cyril's bed, no matter what he says. You will have to run a tab at the grocery. I'm sure Celestia Ann will be willing to help, and Damaris. If Annis has nightmares she likes to crawl into bed with Fan—"

"I'm quite sure Millie can figure these things out," Stuart said. "Millie, I do want you to take the children to Dr. Chetwood and have them vaccinated as soon as possible. We don't want to take any chances with the pox. Now, my dear, let's take care of your patients." He winked at Millie, and ushered Marcia inside. Millie stood staring at the door while the reality of her situation sank in. Now her knees felt wobbly and she wished she had something to lean on. *At Roselands the food was prepared by Phoebe, the laundry was done by several maids, and all of my dresses were sewn by a seamstress in town. Running a household is a great deal of work. Mamma seems to work from sunup to bedtime without a break, even when I'm helping her.*

"Do we have to go with her?" Jed asked. His voice brought Millie back to the present with a jolt. Whatever her troubles were, there were others with more serious difficulties.

"No," Gavriel said, "we don't need charity." Millie was sure there was worry in Gavriel's eyes and something else—fear. "We don't need charity," she repeated, as if she could convince herself by saying the words more loudly.

Millie turned away from the gate. "It won't be charity, I assure you. I will need all the help you can give. I have seven brothers and sisters waiting for me at home."

"Seven! You poor thing!" The officer shook his head.

"Jed and Jaz would make *nine*," Gavriel pointed out.

A Heavy Heart

The guard's eyebrows went up and he whistled. "Nine! Lady, that's a passel of kids. I've got three, and that's more than enough for the missus."

"I'm not sure how much help I could be," Gavriel shook her head. "We would only add to your troubles."

Jed and Jaz were looking up at their sister, eyes wide. Millie was sure they had nowhere else to go. *How can the girl be so stubborn?* Millie thought. "It can't be any harder than stopping a runaway stagecoach, can it? If we can do that together, we can do anything," Millie said with a soft smile.

"You stopped a runaway stagecoach?" The officer leaned on his musket. "Now that's a story I'd like to hear."

Millie looked at the man in exasperation. "With all due respect, sir, this is a private conversation. Let's discuss this on the way back to the station downtown," she said, turning to Gavriel. "We will have to make arrangements for the trunks, in any event."

"Have mercy, ladies," he called after them. "It's boring standing around here all day! What happened on the stagecoach?"

By the time they reached the station it was agreed that the Mikolaus family would travel with Millie to Pleasant Plains and stay at least until Stuart and Marcia returned. Millie arranged for her father's trunk to be delivered to Aunt Wealthy's house and secured seats on the next day's stagecoach as well. When she explained the change of plans to the stationmaster, he ordered a cab to take them to the Hartleys and insisted on paying for it himself.

"Any relation of Miss Wealthy Stanhope," he said, "is a friend of mine. Miss Stanhope nursed my wife through a fever last year. We've been sorry to hear of her troubles."

Millie's Steadfast Love

Bea greeted Millie with squeals and hugs, punctuated with assurances that the Hartleys had room for them all. Bea's mother was one of those women whose heart was as large as her house. She could always find a corner for someone needing comfort. Rooms were prepared and a late tea set before Millie even had a chance to explain.

"Don't you think you're not just as welcome as Millie," Mrs. Hartley said to Gavriel as she poured peppermint tea. "Wealthy Stanhope is an icon in this town. There was practically an armed insurrection the day the mayor closed her house. That's why that awful man has been set to guard it — to keep us out. But they can't keep our gifts away. I send fresh fruit and vegetables every day. Mrs. Wiggles sends soup and bread. Oh, and there are many others. They are living like kings in that house, I assure you. Kings who are very ill, of course, but kings nonetheless." She paused. "Do you suppose kings suffer just as the rest of us do?" she asked.

Mr. Hartley, who was reading a paper in the corner, shook it once. "Yes, dear," he said without looking up.

"I suppose they must," she sighed. "The whole town is storming the gates of Heaven with prayers for her."

"Thank you," Millie said, tears filling her eyes. It was hard to leave Aunt Wealthy to God's care, even if her parents were staying to help.

One of the blessings of being at the Hartleys' was that Mrs. Hartley and Bea provided all the conversation necessary. All that was required of guests was that they smile and nod. Millie was thankful for that now. Bea was so overjoyed at seeing Millie so unexpectedly that she couldn't stop talking and asking her questions. Millie's heart was too torn to talk about Roselands, and talking of the stagecoach ride only made her uncomfortable. So she just smiled and nodded her way through the evening.

Mr. Hartley, who had long since become accustomed to the atmosphere of having females talking and laughing, shook his paper and said, "Yes, dear," every now and then, even if no one had said anything at all. The Mikolauses were uncomfortable at first, sitting very stiff in their chairs. But as Mrs. Hartley went on and on, and the laughter rang out heartily, they began to relax. Mrs. Hartley finished discussing Aunt Wealthy before she turned her attention to the three strangers sitting at her table.

"Isn't she precious, Bea?" she asked, indicating Jaz. "It doesn't take a bit of imagination to believe the child has royal blood in her veins. Why, she looks just like a princess from that exotic book—what was it called?"

"*Arabian Nights*, Mother," Bea said.

"That's the one. I can just see her riding on an elephant. She's simply elegant. And you too, dear," she said, including Gavriel.

"Gavi," Jaz said, looking up at her sister, "am I a princess?"

"Oh, my!" Mrs. Hartley said before Gavi could answer. "Do you love Jesus?" Jaz nodded at her solemnly. "Then of course you are a princess, my dear! God is our Father, isn't He?" Jaz nodded again. "And He is the King of everything. If you are His child, that makes you a princess!"

"Thank you so much for letting us stay, Mrs. Hartley," Millie sighed, as Jaz digested her new princess status. "I don't know what we would have done without you."

"Nonsense," Mrs. Hartley said. "You are always welcome here, Millie Keith. We're all worried out of our heads about Wealthy, as I have said. I wish I could go see her."

"Haven't you been vaccinated?"

"Yes, oh, my yes," Mrs. Hartley said as Bea passed a plate of cookies. Jed took two before Gavriel caught his eyes. He started to put one back, but she shook her head, so he stuffed one in his mouth and the other in his pocket. "Mayor Johnson's daughter died of the pox. She contracted it from a baby blanket that had been used by a sick child. He's afraid the disease will somehow be carried on anything that leaves the house."

"I think that is ridiculous," Bea said.

"That's because you've never lived through a pox epidemic, dear," her mother said. "They are horrible. Millie, can I convince you to stay with us until your parents are able to come home? We have room for you all."

"Yes, Millie, stay!" Bea pleaded. "You can't imagine how lonely it has been. I haven't anyone to talk to anymore," she sighed. "Annabeth is a married lady, away on a honeymoon with her husband, and Camilla has gone to university to pursue her studies." Millie was glad to hear that. Years ago she and Camilla had dreamed of finishing school and attending a college together. "I never thought that I would be left here all alone." Bea's big blue eyes were sad and her cupid lips pouted.

"All alone?" Millie couldn't help but laugh. "I cannot believe that, Bea. How many parties did you attend last week?"

"Three. No, four. But they were no fun at all, I assure you. If it wasn't for Jason Pinkert, they would have been very dull indeed." Bea launched into detailed descriptions of not only the parties, but each dress she had worn. While her mother nodded in agreement, the two young Mikolaus children ate cookies and Gavi sipped her tea.

A Heavy Heart

"Oh!" Bea said at last. "Look at the time! And I have not even begun to describe Annabeth's wedding!" Jed was sitting on his hands, Jaz was fidgeting, and Gavriel's eyes had a decidedly glazed look to them by the time the wedding had been described in minute detail. Bea and Mrs. Hartley practically tripped over each other's words in their excitement. The darkness had settled outside the windows and the night sounds of insects had begun before the two finally seemed exhausted of conversation.

"Now, Bea," Mrs. Hartley said at last, "we must not weary our guests with talk. It's time for bed." The Hartleys had two guest rooms. One had been made up for Millie, Gavriel, and Jasmine, complete with a small princess bed for Jaz. The other had been prepared for Jedidiah. Mrs. Hartley bid them good night at the door. Gavriel shut it and leaned against it.

"Do they always talk this much?" she whispered.

"Ever since I have known them," Millie said, smiling. "Bea is growing more like her mother every day."

Gavriel helped Jaz prepare for bed, slipping a nightgown over her head and braiding her long, dark hair. She held the little girl on her lap and whispered a prayer with her, obviously uncomfortable praying in front of company. Millie pretended to be occupied with her Bible.

"Gavi?" the little girl asked, as her sister tucked her in the baby bed that had been brought for her. "Am I really, really a princess?"

"Of course you are," Gavriel said, kissing her brow.

"That's good," Jaz said sleepily. "What's an elephant?"

"The wildest beast you can imagine," Gavriel said. "They live in the jungles and trample anyone who gets in their way. But when a *true* princess taps on an elephant's leg and commands in a very royal voice 'Pick me up!', the elephant leans down and lets her climb up its trunk to sit on its back. Then he carries her wherever she wishes to go. Now close your eyes, and maybe you will find a dream elephant."

" 'Night," the little girl said happily.

"Good night, Millie," Gavriel said, after her own hair was brushed and braided.

Millie snuggled into her side of the huge feather bed. The fresh, clean sheets wrapped around her like a sweet-smelling cloud. She had almost forgotten how wonderful a soft, clean bed could be after all the public beds at the stagecoach way stations. And in just about a week she would be home in her own bed. Millie drifted toward sleep, praying for Charles, her brothers and sisters, little Elsie Dinsmore and Cousin Horace, Luke, and Laylie. And princess Jaz as well. *Jesus, I've read all about princesses in books. If belonging to You makes me a princess, then I think the authors got it all wrong. Storybook princesses never have to do a thing but wait for the prince to sweep them off their feet. I think I like Your story better, Lord. I like excitement, travel, and adventure. But I wouldn't mind a bit if You included a Prince Charles in my story. Charming!* Millie shook her head. *I meant Prince Charming. Really, Lord. Time to pray about something else. . . . Lord, bless Mamma and Pappa for being so good. Help Mamma get the rest she needs and don't let Aunt Wealthy die —*

Suddenly the old house groaned, its timbers cooling with the night, and Millie was afraid, just as she had been as a child. It was as if a door had opened, and a dark, horrible giant had crept into the room. She was wide awake, but Gavriel and Jaz slept peacefully.

Aunt Wealthy might die! Surely God wouldn't allow it! He saved Fan's life when everyone prayed, but other people have died. Little

A Heavy Heart

Elsie's mamma died. Many people in Pleasant Plains died when the ague was so bad, and Mr. Jones . . . Millie's mind was filled with the vision of his stiff face and staring eyes. She shuddered. *Lord, help Aunt Wealthy! Please!* she prayed. *Make her well.* Millie tried to have faith, but the pictures wouldn't leave her mind, and the creeping feeling of fear seemed to fill the corners of the room. *What if Aunt Wealthy does die? What if something terrible happens to one of the children? I'm not as wise as Pappa thinks I am. I should've told him about all my doubts.*

Millie crept out of the bed and groped for her Bible. She curled up on the window seat, where the moonlight was bright enough for reading, but no verse of all the Scriptures she had memorized came to mind. She opened her Bible and stabbed her finger down, then read the verse under it: "But he will reply, 'I don't know you, or where you came from! Away from me, you evildoers!' " Millie shook her head.

Lord, I need help! she prayed and tried again. *"That same day he removed all the male goats that were streaked or spotted, and all the speckled or spotted female goats (all that had white on them) and all the dark colored lambs, and he placed them in the care of his sons."*

Millie groaned. *What does that mean? Nothing. Think of a word, any word. That's what Pappa had said. Wisdom. I need wisdom.* She turned to the concordance and ran her finger down the page until she found the word *wisdom*. There were a lot of Scriptures listed, so she picked one in Proverbs 8, beginning at verse 1. *"Does not wisdom call out? Does not understanding raise her voice? On the heights along the way, where the paths meet, she takes her stand; beside the gates leading into the city, at the entrances, she cries aloud: 'To you, O men, I call out; I raise my voice to all mankind. You who are simple, gain prudence; you who are foolish, gain understanding.' "*

Millie's Steadfast Love

Lord, these words are sweet, like honey cakes when I'm very hungry.
Millie kept reading, pausing often to go back and re-read
verse 15: *"By me kings reign and rulers make laws that are just; by
me princes govern, and all nobles who rule on earth. I love those who
love me, and those who seek me find me."*

*Mamma and Pappa were wise. They sought the wisdom of the Lord
for their children every day.* She read on, feeling more and more
at peace, loving the poetry of the words. *"I was appointed from
eternity, from the beginning, before the world began .... I was there
when he set the heavens in place.... I was the craftsman at his side. I
was filled with delight day after day, rejoicing always in his presence,
rejoicing in his whole world and delighting in mankind."*

Millie smiled at the picture of God creating the world
and mankind, with Wisdom rejoicing like a dancer at His
side. She kept reading through Proverbs chapter 8, and
on into chapter 9. In verse 10 she read, *"The fear of the
LORD is the beginning of wisdom, and knowledge of the Holy One
is understanding."* Millie stopped. *"The fear of the LORD is the
beginning of wisdom."* Her mother had taught her that fear
of the Lord was different from the fear she'd felt just min-
utes before. It was reverence and awe at how mighty and
wonderful God was. It came from understanding who He
was and what He had done. Millie read the second part of
the line. *"Knowledge of the Holy One is understanding."*

Now a memory verse did come to mind, as if the Holy
Spirit were testifying to the truth of Proverbs 9:10 and
comforting her all at once: *"I am convinced that neither death
nor life, neither angels nor demons, neither the present nor the
future, nor any powers, neither height nor depth, nor anything else
in all creation, will be able to separate us from the love of God that
is in Christ Jesus our Lord."*

A Heavy Heart

Jesus is the Holy One of God. He died for Aunt Wealthy and He is not going to fail her now. Not even if she goes home to Him.

Millie closed her Bible and bowed her head. "Thank You, Jesus," she prayed. The fear that had been creeping into the corners of the room was gone, replaced by a quiet excitement. *Bad things do happen. But God set the oceans in their places and the stars in the sky, and Wisdom laughed when He did. Surely God can take care of Millie Keith, and Aunt Wealthy, and all of His children, no matter what happens.*

"Are you sure you can make the journey by yourself?" Mrs. Hartley asked at breakfast the next morning. "I heard the most horrible story at the bakery this morning while I was waiting in line. Everyone was talking about a stagecoach that was coming over the mountains. The driver fell dead! I know this is unbelievable, but Mrs. Clondike swears that it's true. Her son-in-law was on the stagecoach!" Millie and Gavriel exchanged glances. There had been only two men on the stagecoach, Stuart Keith and Alexander Lyone, and neither one of them was Mrs. Clondike's son-in-law. "The passengers barely escaped with their lives. But I'm sure you have no need to worry. There are no real mountains between here and Pleasant Plains."

"Oh, Mother," Bea said, rolling her eyes. "You shouldn't believe everything you hear. Besides, don't you think it strange that exciting adventures always happen to someone Mrs. Clondike knows? If these things do happen, it is other people that they happen to, not you or your very best friends. I'm sure Millie will be perfectly safe."

Millie's Steadfast Love

"God will be with us every mile of our journey, no matter what happens," Millie assured them, giving Mrs. Hartley a kiss. "But if we don't hurry, that stage is going to leave without us."

⁓

It took nine days for them to reach Pleasant Plains, and though Jaz amused everyone they met by explaining that she was a princess on her way to find an elephant, Millie soon realized that Gavriel shared very little about herself. She did discover that Jedidiah loved to read. He devoured her serial by Dickens and any other reading material he could find. When she saw him struggling with a stick of charcoal and a piece of butcher's paper he had begged for in one of the many towns they passed through, she offered the use of the small lap desk her father had purchased for her when she began her journey from Pleasant Plains. Jedidiah was absorbed in his writing, scratching away at the page or gazing into space, but when Millie asked to read what he had written, he quickly put his hand over the page. "I don't like people to see it," he said, his face reddening at his own rudeness. "I'm still working on my spelling. It's not very good, and I have to use a lot of words that I'm not sure of to tell the story right. But I can read it."

"I have a brother named Cyril," Millie said, "whose spelling is not very good either. Perhaps you would like to take lessons with him?"

"If we can stay long enough . . . " He glanced at his older sister, then fell silent.

The miles rolled endlessly past the cultivated fields and farms of Ohio into dense forests of hickory, walnut, and sassafras trees. Jaz and Jed were fascinated by everything Millie pointed out. The sketchbook she had kept since leaving home was the occasion of much mirth for them, and they tried to guess what each drawing represented. Jaz and Jed had traveled far enough south to be familiar with armadillos and so recognized them immediately, but they had never seen an alligator, and Jed insisted on writing down everything Millie said about them. She pointed out the various species of birds they could see through the windows and even tried to draw a few.

"God does it better," Jaz said one day, as Millie attempted a Steller's jay.

"He certainly does," Millie laughed, trying to figure out why the bird's beak was not right. "And a man named Audubon does it better too. When we get to Pleasant Plains, I'll show you some of his pictures in a big, beautiful book."

Jed was fascinated by Millie's prayer journal as well, though she explained that it was very private. By the end of the week, Millie still did not know where her new friends had come from or what in the world they were afraid of, but she was sure that God had a plan in sending them to Pleasant Plains.

CHAPTER

7

Changes at Home

*See, I am doing a new thing!
Now it springs up; do you
not perceive it?*

ISAIAH 43:19

Changes at Home

*B*lue smoke and the smell of saltpeter hung in the still air the day they arrived in Pleasant Plains. Millie was just as glad that they had missed the big Fourth of July celebration the day before. The cannons would have roared all day, and the constant bang of firecrackers would have unsettled animals and babies alike.

"Why, Millie Keith!" Gordon Lightcap exclaimed as he helped her down from the stagecoach with such a warm look in his eyes that Millie blushed. "It's about time! We've been expecting you for at least two days. A driver came through with the most outrageous story of a girl single-handedly stopping a runaway stagecoach. Rhoda Jane looked up at me and said, 'Millie's on her way!'" Gordon chuckled and shook his head.

"It was not single-handedly, Gordon. I would like to present Gavriel Mikolaus, the other 'daring maiden' stagecoach stopper. We were only doing what had to be done," said Millie.

"You mean it's true, Millie? I thought it was just one of those things they pass down the line like the giant stage-attacking bear." Gordon pulled off his cap and bowed to Gavriel. "Any friend of Millie Keith is welcome in Pleasant Plains."

"This is Gavi's brother, Jedidiah, and her sister, Jasmine," said Millie, finishing the introduction.

Gordon greeted them both and then said, "Well? Is someone going to tell me about the runaway stagecoach, or are you going to leave me in suspense?"

"You will have to suffer," Millie said. "I don't want to tell it more than once, so I'll wait until we're all together at Keith Hill."

"And where are your parents?" Gordon suddenly realized that all of the passengers had gotten off and the two of them were missing. "I thought they were coming home with you?"

Millie explained about the smallpox at Aunt Wealthy's house as Gordon started stripping the harness from the far leader, working mostly with his left hand. Gavriel set her carpetbag down and started loosening the far leader's gear.

Gordon gave her one of his dazzling smiles. "There's no need to help me, miss," he said, holding up his crippled right hand. "It's ugly, but it hardly slows me down at all. You can go up to the station with the others. We'll be right along."

"I wasn't helping you," Gavi said, flushing. "I was helping the horses."

"Oh," Gordon nodded. "In that case, I'm not the one who needs to give permission. What do you say, boys? Do you want the lady to help you?"

The far leader pawed at the ground and snorted. "Well, then," Gordon laughed, "who am I to tell you no?"

"What happened to your hand?" Jed asked.

"This?" He waved his claw at the boy. "I was tamping down the powder in my muzzleloader and I leaned on the rod like so," he demonstrated, using a shovel handle as the ramrod. "The powder went off, shooting the rod through my hand and into my chest."

"That's terrible!" Gavi said, looking up at him before starting on the wheeler's gear.

"You would think so." Gordon went back to work, moving twice as fast to catch up with her. "But it was wonderful, really. I was lying on my cot with the rod jerking to the beat of my heart—and old Doc Chetwood sure I was going

to die—when God spoke to me for the first time. He used
Millie Keith's voice, but it was Him all right. He just told
her what to say. 'For I am the Lord, your God, who takes
hold of your right hand and says to you, Do not fear; I will
help you.'" He glanced at Millie and smiled, then asked
Gavriel, "Are you staying in Pleasant Plains, or will you be
traveling on, Miss Mikolaus?"

"Staying," Millie said when Gavi hesitated. "They will be
staying at our house, Gordon. Speaking of which," she
turned quickly around to Gavriel, "would you mind waiting here while I gather up my brothers and sisters from the
neighbors where they've been staying? Ru is at the house,
I think, but he doesn't know we're coming."

"Don't worry about a thing," Gordon said. "I'll bring
them over in the wagon when I deliver your trunks. They
can have biscuits and talk to Rhoda Jane here at the station
until then."

Millie had no more than stepped in the door when Rhoda
Jane grabbed her around the neck. "Millie! I have missed
you so much! I am dying to hear all about your adventures."

"Come over for supper," Millie suggested. "And bring
Gordon with you."

"I'll try," Rhoda Jane said. "Mother's mind has gotten so
bad, she's not even able to help with the station now. We
have another stage coming through, and if there are no passengers, then I'll be able to get away. If there are, I'll need
to stay and cook for them, of course. Where are your
mother and father?"

Millie explained again about the smallpox and Aunt
Wealthy. She turned to Gavriel and said, "Rhoda Jane is one
of my dearest friends, Gavi. And she is Gordon's sister—the

one you just met outside with the horses." She turned back to Rhoda Jane and introduced Gavriel. "Rhoda Jane, I'd like you to meet Gavriel Mikolaus." Gavriel nodded, then shyly looked away.

"Pleased to meet you," said Rhoda Jane, smiling as she wiped her hands on her apron.

"Do you know where the children are staying?" Millie asked. "I had no time to find out, but Pleasant Plains is so small, I doubt they can hide for long."

"That's true," Rhoda Jane laughed. "Your mother parceled them out two by two. Cyril and Don are with us, but they begged to go fishing this afternoon and Gordon let them because they helped shovel the stables yesterday. I'll send them along as soon as they get back. Ru is at Keith Hill, Zillah and Adah are staying with the Monockers, and Mrs. Prior is keeping Fan and little Annis over at the hotel."

"I'll collect them on my way," Millie said. "Gavriel is going to wait here with you for now. Gordon said he would bring her and her younger brother and sister over later."

Millie left Gavi and Rhoda Jane talking and started across town. *Pleasant Plains has hardly grown at all since I left.* There was one more building in town, a small house that she knew from her mother's letters was the new home of Nicholas and Damaris Ransquate. The streets were still sandy with blowing sand piled against the west sides of buildings, but most of the stores had a fresh coat of paint and the whole town looked bright and inviting. Millie saw Fan and Annis as soon as she stepped into the lobby of the Union Hotel. Her youngest sisters were playing dolls in the corner. Fan had a pink bow in her hair and looked very ladylike. Annis, who was still four, didn't look like a baby anymore. Millie had not realized how much she missed them until this very moment.

Fan glanced up at the sound of the door. "Sister Millie!" Fan squealed. Annis looked up from her dolls, but she didn't have time to move before Millie fell to her knees and gathered them in her arms.

"What on earth is this racket out here?" Mrs. Prior asked, coming into the room. "Millie Keith! My stars, I wasn't expecting you yet." Millie explained about her mother staying in Lansdale, and Mrs. Prior looked concerned. "You're sure you can handle all the children now?" she asked. "You could leave the little girls with me until your mother returns."

"Quite sure!" Millie said, taking her sisters' hands. "I have missed them too much to leave them. But if I have any trouble, I will call on you."

"Do that," Mrs. Prior said. "I know how to keep them in line. You have a whole town here to help you if you call!"

Millie thanked her again, and taking one sister by each hand, she started up the street. They had gone only a few yards when Fan's hand wiggled out of hers. The little girl pulled the bow from her hair and stuck it in her apron pocket, then sat down in the sand.

"What are you doing?" Millie asked.

"My boots are too tight," Fan explained, pulling at the laces.

"They bite her feet," Annis said.

"Pinch my feet," Fan corrected. "So I'm taking them off."

"Would Mamma let you walk through town barefoot?" Millie asked.

"They hurt, Millie! Mamma won't mind. She said we can't have new shoes till frost this year."

"Oh, all right," Millie said. "But I don't think I can carry you all the way home."

"That's all right," Fan said. "I like bare toes best." She stuck one boot in each of her apron pockets, then took Millie's hand again.

"Guess what?" Fan said as they turned the corner. "Celestia Ann says a baby is coming to stay with her!"

"Really!" Millie said with a smile. "When will the baby come to visit?"

"Next month," Fan said. "But it's not visiting, silly. It's coming to stay."

"It's going to stay," Annis said happily.

"What I want to know," Fan said, "is where is it coming from?" She looked up at Millie.

"You can ask Mamma that when she gets home," Millie said.

"I told Emmaretta Lightcap that I wanted a baby to come stay with me, but she said babies can't come stay until you're a married lady. She said Rhoda Jane told her that. Zillah is going to marry Wallace Ormsby; then lots of babies can stay with her."

"Zillah is too young to get married," Millie said, feeling a blush creep up her face.

"She is so going to marry him." Fan kicked at a rock with her bare toe. "Ouch. I heard Zillah and Adah talking about it. Zillah said she'd leave me in the swamp if I told anybody."

"Pappa said not to go there," Annis chirped happily.

"He said babies like you can't go there," Fan said, glaring at her.

"I don't want either one of you going near the swamp," Millie said firmly, glad the subject had changed.

Changes at Home

Next they collected Adah and Zillah from the Monocker house. Millie was surprised at how they had grown. Zillah was only an inch shorter than Millie and had the form of a graceful young lady. Adah had grown tall but seemed to be all angles, elbows, and knees.

"Mamma and Pappa aren't with you?" Zillah asked uncertainly when Millie explained the situation. "Perhaps we should stay with the Monockers until they return."

"I'm quite sure that Pappa expects us all to stay at the house," Millie said. "And it will take all of us to keep the place running until they arrive."

Mr. Monocker insisted on driving Millie and her sisters home in his new surrey. People waved and called to Millie, welcoming her home, until the surrey began to make the long climb up Keith Hill. The trees and roses Ru had planted had all grown, and Millie looked in confusion at the young man who opened the gate for the carriage, only to realize it was Ru.

A loose-boned hound bayed at them from the porch, but his stub of a tail belied his bark by wagging furiously.

"Bobforshort!" Millie said. "We've met before, do you remember?"

"We call him Bob now," Ru explained with a shrug, "for short." The tiny pup Uncle Horace had purchased at a way station when he had traveled to Pleasant Plains the year before had grown into an enormous beast, but his tail was still only half as long as it should have been. Mr. Monocker bade them good-bye and Millie followed Ru inside.

The house that had seemed so spacious and elegant after her stay in the warehouse now seemed small and rather simply furnished, but Millie had never been so glad to see any four walls in her life.

"You've changed," Ru said, regarding her critically. "You're prettier and . . . "

"And more stylish!" Zillah said.

"And you!" Millie told her sister. "You are so grown-up!"

"I *am* thirteen, after all," Zillah said, blushing.

"You have all grown," Millie went on, glancing around the circle.

"Is Aunt Wealthy going to be all right?" Adah asked.

"I think she will," Millie said. "Mamma and Pappa are taking care of her, and the whole city of Lansdale seems to be praying for her."

Millie's brother and sisters looked at her silently for a moment; then everyone seemed to start talking at once.

"Are you all well now?"

"Tell us about Elsie . . . "

"Was slavery really as bad as . . . "

"What happened to Laylie?"

"Were the parties marvelous?" This last question was from Zillah.

"I am completely well, but can't possibly answer you all at once," Millie laughed. "So Annis may ask first." Annis looked up at her sister with big, solemn eyes, and shook her head. "Well, then," Millie said. "I think I'll have to let Fan go next."

"What happened to Laylie?" Fan asked. "Mamma read us your letters and we have been praying for her every single night."

"I don't know," Millie said. "She escaped, but we'll have to trust Jesus that He's taking care of her."

"What about little Elsie?" Adah asked. "I don't think she should stay at Roselands. It sounds like a horrible place."

"It's a wonderful place," Millie said, "and Uncle Horace is a good man. But Aunt Isabel . . . " She felt the words catch in her throat. Mamma wouldn't want her speaking ill of her aunt, and neither would Jesus. "We will continue praying for little Elsie," Millie said, "and all of the Dinsmores."

"You sound just like Mamma," Adah laughed. "I think we should steal Elsie and bring her here."

"I would be willing to take Elsie's place!" Zillah said. Everyone looked at her and she flushed. "She is very rich. It must be nice to have houses and lands and servants to look after you. Look!" She caught up Millie's hand and held it up next to her own. Millie was surprised at the difference. Zillah's hand was callused from helping Ru in the garden, and the knuckles were red from washing dishes and clothes. Millie's was soft and white. "You've been gone almost a year, Millie, and you have changed so much! You're stylish and beautiful. I would give anything to look like you!"

"The rich people in the South have slaves," Ru pointed out. "You wouldn't want that, Zil."

"But some rich people are good," Zillah said.

"That's true," Millie agreed. "Mrs. Travilla was wonderful. And little Elsie is just as sweet as she can be."

"She's just a baby," Fan said. "Maybe she'll get bad by the time she grows up."

"Well," Millie said, sitting down and pulling Annis up onto her lap. "I think I am richer than Elsie Dinsmore."

"You do?" Fan said.

"Oh, yes. Elsie has no brothers or sisters. Her poor mamma's dead and she has never seen her pappa."

"Poor little Elsie," Fan said. "Why can't she come here, Millie? We'd take care of her!"

"I'm glad to hear you say that," Millie said. "Because God has sent us someone to care for. Three someones, in fact." Millie explained about the three Mikolauses, as her brother and sisters listened intently.

"Of course they can stay," Ru said. "Jedidiah can take my room if he likes. It's the best we have. I'll sleep in the loft."

"They're coming!" Zillah said. "I see Gordon's wagon."

The Keiths trooped out to the porch as the wagon drew near. Don was sitting in the back. He jumped down and ran straight for Millie. She had another shock—her little brother was taller than Zillah!

"Millie!" he said, and his voice broke. He cleared his throat and tried again. "You look different. Shiny and clean-like."

"I have always been clean!" Millie said, grabbing him and giving him a hug, to his apparent disgust. "Where's Cyril?"

"He's still fishing. I left him to come back and get some bait, but I found out that you were home, so I came along with Gordon."

Ru and Gordon carried the trunks inside and up the stairs. They came back down to find everyone settled into the parlor. The Mikolauses were looking at the Keiths, and the Keiths were studying the Mikolauses. Gordon smiled at them all.

"Rhoda Jane couldn't come," said Gordon. "She has guests to take care of. But she said not to worry about supper tomorrow night. She's going to put together a welcome-home-Millie potluck. Everyone is eager to see you, Millie, and to hear about your trip."

Suddenly, something big bounded in the window. Cyril was breathing hard, and twigs and leaves were stuck in his hair. His overalls were ripped where they weren't patched, and he had forgotten his shirt. Millie wasn't sure whether he looked like a man or a beast.

"Hey!" he said, smiling at the roomful of people and scratching his head. "I just heard you were home, Millie, and I thought I could beat you here and get cleaned up."

Jasmine stood up and walked over to him. She gazed up at him for a moment, then tapped his leg.

"Pick me up," she commanded. Cyril grinned, and scooped her into his arms.

"Take me over there." He followed the little pointing finger, setting her down on top of the table. "Good!" she said, patting his cheeks. "Good boy! You will be my best elephant."

CHAPTER

8

The Princess and the Pachyderm

For I was hungry and you gave me something to eat, I was thirsty and you gave me something to drink, I was a stranger and you invited me in.

MATTHEW 25:35

yril's face turned as red as his hair. "I'm not an elephant," he said. "I'm a human-type being. Look, two legs," he stomped his feet, "no trunk. My name is Cyril. I'm a boy." Jaz's eyes filled with tears and her lower lip trembled.

"Cyril!" Fan said. "You made her cry!"

"I didn't do anything!" he insisted.

Huge tears rolled over Jaz's eyelashes and splashed down her cheeks.

"Don't cry, little girl," Don said. "I'll be your elephant."

"You're *not* my elephant!" Jaz cried harder.

Millie was sure it must have something to do with the leaves and mud; apart from these, Cyril and Don were identical.

"Oh, all right," said Cyril, looking even more embarrassed. "I'll be an elephant. Just stop crying!"

"Pick me up!" Jaz demanded. Cyril shrugged and bent down to pick her up. She took him by the ears and looked deep into his eyes. "Take me to Mamma, elephant," she said.

Cyril cut his eyes to Millie.

"She's a princess," Millie explained. "Elephants take princesses wherever they want to go."

Gavriel took Jaz from Cyril's arms. "I'm sorry, Jaz," she said. "Not even elephants can walk to Heaven."

"Is it too high?" Jaz asked.

"Much too high, baby," said Gavi.

"I'm not a baby," Jaz wiggled out of her arms. "I don't want you, Gavi. I want Mamma!"

The look on Gavriel's face tore Millie's heart. "Our mother and father are dead," Gavriel explained in a flat voice. "Jaz doesn't understand what that means yet. She keeps thinking we are going to find them."

Fan wrapped her arms protectively around Jaz. "Cyril," Fan said, "you made an *orphan* princess cry!" Annis hugged Jaz from the other side, and both little girls glared at Cyril.

"We are just staying long enough to earn some money to go on," Gavi said, obviously uncomfortable with the sympathy she saw around her. "Millie asked me to help until your parents return, but I can see that—"

"Of course you're going to stay," Gordon said. "Millie needs all the help she can get." Millie sincerely hoped that she was not as helpless as that made her sound, but she knew Gordon's heart was in the right place.

"Besides," Ru said logically, "money is a hard thing to come by in Pleasant Plains just now."

Jaz's sniffles were loud in the silence.

"Cyril," Fan whispered, "do something! She's still crying."

"I don't know what to do," Cyril whispered back. "I'm no good with princesses."

"Has Ru showed you around, Millie?" Gordon asked. "He has done wonders with the gardens this spring and summer." Millie smiled thankfully at him.

"Why don't you come with us, Gavriel?" she said. "I'm sure Jaz would like to see the animals."

"I'm sure she would, too," Gavi said.

Fan took one of the princess's hands and Annis the other, and they led her toward the door.

The flower gardens around the house were wonderful, but the vegetable gardens were Ru's pride and joy. He explained each and every plant and plot in detail. Millie tried to pay attention, but the smells of Keith Hill, the sweet garden flowers, the freshly turned dirt, the hay curing in the barn, even the animal smell of the barnyard, were flooding her with memories of her family. She could imagine them laughing and talking, building and planting, and making a life in Pleasant Plains. And somewhere beneath it all, like a whisper on the breeze, was the delicious wildness of the Kankakee Marsh where she loved to walk alone and talk to God. This was home, and she had missed it more than she could say. *What if I had married Charles and stayed in the South? Would I ever have stopped missing this place and these people?*

They had reached the squash patch when Millie was called back to the present by the gagging noises Cyril was making in his throat. Ru ignored him. He plucked a squash bug off a leaf and crushed it between his fingers.

"That's disgusting," Adah said. "Why do you have to do that?"

"Because the weather has been hot and not too dry," Ru said with perfect gardener's logic. "Good for squash and squash bugs, too."

"Look, Millie," Don said. "These are mine." He pulled her to a corner of the garden that was almost obscured by a leafy tangle of vines. He pulled aside a leaf to reveal a large green pumpkin.

"See, princess?" Fan said. "Don's growing pies!" Jaz hiccuped. She hadn't smiled since her long-sought elephant had failed her. Cyril kept glancing at her and glancing away. Jaz just watched him with big, sad eyes, but Fan frowned at him, as if she expected him to have done better.

"Soon as frost comes, we're not going to eat anything but pumpkin pie till Christmas," Don agreed. "And we're gonna use Cyril's honey to sweeten it!"

Millie's Steadfast Love

"Honey!" Millie said in surprise. "You have bees, Cyril?"

"I've got bees!" Cyril said, smacking his forehead. "You folks just go on with your tour. I'll be back!" He ran down the hill toward the river, Bob galloping after him.

"Is he going somewhere important?" Gavi asked. "He certainly seems in a hurry."

"He's Cyril," Ru said, as if that explained it. They watched until he disappeared behind the springhouse at the foot of the hill, then Ru went on with his tour.

"Ru has really transformed the place, Millie," said Gordon, smiling proudly and looking around. "Last fall, if you wanted to see him, you had to come looking out here in the garden." Gordon laughed heartily as he patted Ru on the back.

Ru nodded and was about to move on to his onion patch when Cyril reappeared. "Cy's been swimming in his clothes again!" Annis said, pointing.

Even from the top of the garden Millie could see that her brother was sopping wet. His hair was plastered down and his overalls clung to his legs, but he didn't seem to notice. He was advancing on what appeared to be two small haystacks at the bottom of the garden, with a jar in one hand and a stick in the other. Bob was right at his heels.

"What's he doing?" Millie asked.

"He's after honey," Ru explained. "Those are the hives he made for his bees. He must have jumped in the river to wash off the sweat. He says the bees only like clean people."

"Your scent has to be neutral or they won't let you anywhere near the hive," added Gordon.

Cyril stopped and pointed his finger at Bobforshort, who's half-tail dropped between his legs. The dog slunk back to stand by Fan as Cyril went on to his hives. Millie watched in fascination as Cyril knelt by the small pile of hay and reached inside. Even from this distance she could see a cloud of bees around him, and it made her a little queasy. The lump on the end of the stick was black with bees when Cyril pulled it out. He brushed them off with his hand, then dropped the lump in the jar and put the lid on. He held it up and waved at them, then started walking toward the river again. A cloud of bees followed him.

"They smell the honey," Ru said. "He's going down to the river to lose them."

"How did Cyril learn so much about bees?" Millie asked. "Does he have a book?"

Zillah laughed. "Cyril read a book? Not unless Pappa forces him to. He learned from Mr. Vreeland, who runs the ferry."

"Mr. Vreeland's family kept bees in Holland," said Gordon. "He's got generations of knowledge about all of it—everything from building the bee-keeps to harvesting the honey."

Ru's garden tour was completed by the time Cyril caught up with them. He had obviously been in the river again, but he marched straight up to Jaz, bold as a knight in dripping armor, and held out the jar with a chunk of honeycomb inside.

"Gold for the princess," he said with a bow.

Jaz clapped her hands. "Good elephant!"

Cyril's grin seemed to spread from his head to his toes. "Don't go openin' it out here," he said quickly. "The bees will smell it and come to take it back."

"We'll save it for dinner," Gavriel said. She confiscated the jar before Jaz could work the top off and attract any bees.

Millie's Steadfast Love

"How could they take it back?" Millie laughed. "Surely the jar is too heavy for them to carry."

"Shows what you know," said Cyril as he hiked up his wet overalls. "They'd guzzle it up, just like they drink nectar from flowers, and take it back to their hive. They could drink that little piece of comb dry in no time at all."

"Cyril!" Millie had just noticed the red blotches on his chest and arms. "They stung you!"

" 'Course they did," Cyril said. "They're *bees*."

"Doesn't it hurt?" asked Millie, staring at the big welts in dismay.

He shrugged. "Yep. But for a dollar a gallon I can get used to it." He hiked up his wet overalls again. "All you have to do to make money is have something somebody wants," he nodded at the straw hives, "and I have my own little gold mine. I'll probably get three, four gallons from each hive this fall."

"Eight bucks? No fooling?" said Jedidiah. He had been following along quietly, paying little attention to the garden, but he was clearly interested now.

"At least. Ten, if I'm lucky," said Cyril.

"Don't count your money till the honey's sold," Gordon said. "Those bees could decide to swarm tomorrow and leave you with nothing."

"Those little ladies are not leaving me," Cyril said. "I take good care of 'em!"

Next everyone followed Ru to the barn to see the laying hens and Belle, the little milk cow. Their last stop was the pasture fence behind the barn.

"Horsies!" Jaz cried in delight when she caught sight of Inspiration, one of the Keiths' mares. Inspiration whickered and trotted to the fence, reaching over to nibble Fan's ears.

114

"Don't you dare ignore me," Millie laughed, as she leaned across the fence to rub the horse's nose. Before Millie had left for Roselands, Inspiration had been her special pet, carrying her on adventures across the fields and marsh when her lungs were too weak for long walks. The horse stomped at the ground. "I missed you, too," Millie said.

Glory, the Keiths' second mare, trotted from the other side of the pasture to see if any carrots were being distributed. A long-legged foal followed behind her.

"Well, hello," Millie said, as it reached its head through the fence. "Who are you?"

"I forgot you didn't know," Ru said. "Esther's a month old already. Glory must have foaled just about the time you were leaving Roselands to come home."

"Esther means star," Adah explained, "for the star on her forehead." The little filly was shiny black, with three white stockings as well as the star-shaped blaze.

"She's beautiful!" Millie said, rubbing her neck gently. The baby horse snuffled her hand curiously, then grabbed onto her thumb and started sucking. Millie laughed and pulled her hand away.

"We just thought Glory was getting fat," Fan said, "and didn't like to jump fences any more. But what I want to know is—"

"Fan, you know Mamma don't like you talking about such things," Ru said, glancing at Gavi.

"—why we can't ride Esther yet?" Fan continued, ignoring her brother.

"Oh," Ru flushed. "Her ankles are not strong enough yet. You have to wait till she grows up."

"It's about time to start supper," Millie said, turning toward the house.

Millie's Steadfast Love

"Can we stay here, Millie?" Fan asked.

"Yeah, can we?" asked Annis, who was holding Jaz's hand. Fan walked over to the two smaller girls and begged, "I can take care of the princess."

"If Gavriel says it's all right," Millie decided. Three sets of eyes turned to Gavi. Gavi nodded her approval.

"Very well," Millie agreed. "Stay in the pasture where I can see you from the house and come in for dinner as soon as we call. And what are you two up to?" Cyril and Jed jumped. They had been standing just a little apart from the group, heads together, talking seriously.

"No need to scare us like that, Millie," Cyril said. "We were just talking." Before Millie could ask him why he was so easily frightened, Cyril had turned back to Jed. "Come on," he said. "I'll show you my room. You will be staying with me, I expect. We'll have to work something out about the beds." The rest of the group followed Cyril and Jed to the house.

"Why don't you come on up to the house with us, Gordon," Ru said.

They went straight to the kitchen to prepare something to eat for everyone. As she set a fire in the woodstove, Millie glanced out the window to make sure the little girls were within sight.

"Jaz would be happy to stay in the stable with the horses," Gavi said, looking over her shoulder.

"I was thinking that she could stay in Fan and Annis's room," Millie said with a smile. "Jed will stay in the boys' room, and you can have the guest room, Gavi."

Millie pulled one of her mother's aprons from the drawer. Before she could put it on, Gordon took the apron from her and wrapped it around his waist. "What are you doing?" Millie asked.

"Gord," Ru said, "you look like a girl."

"Biscuits, ham, gravy, and mashed potatoes," Gordon said, "don't care who cooks them."

"My taste buds are gonna care," Ru insisted.

"I cook for the passengers at the way station all the time," Gordon pointed out. "You've seen me do it. Millie and Gavriel have been traveling all day, and I am sure they are very tired."

"I should have thought of it first, Gordon," Zillah said. "I'll help."

"Me, too," Adah said.

"Anyone else?" Gordon held out an apron toward Ru.

Ru shook his head and started toward the door. "I've got bugs to squash," he said quickly.

Gordon soon had Adah and Zillah peeling potatoes while he mixed up a pie crust. "Why don't you ladies go sit on the porch swing?" he said to Millie and Gavi. "There's a nice cool breeze out there, and we have everything under control."

"We would love to unpack," Millie said, glancing at Gavi. "If someone would keep an eye on Jaz . . . "

"I can watch them out the window," Zillah assured her.

Millie showed Gavi to the guest room and made sure she didn't need any help unpacking her trunk before she went to her own bedroom. Ru and Gordon had placed her carpetbag at the foot of the bed. *I'm home! My own bed, my own room, my own walls!* Millie sighed and sank down on her bed. She lay back and looked around the familiar room with a smile. *These surroundings are so different from the elegant rooms at Roselands,* Millie thought wistfully. *Roselands seems like a thousand miles and a thousand years from here now. And Charles is a thousand miles away.* Millie suddenly sat straight up. She took her Bible and the small tin box that held Charles's rose from the carpetbag. She swallowed hard to keep back the tears as she set them on her night table by the bed. *Does Charles even know where Pleasant Plains is—how far away I am? Will I ever hear from him again?* She set her lips in determination, took the rose from the table, and slid open the top drawer, shutting the rose firmly inside. *Lord, I must stop allowing my thoughts to drift to Charles.*

Millie strode from her room with resolve and went in search of Gavi. Gavi had just finished unpacking her small trunk when Millie appeared in the doorway. "Let's go and sit on the swing," Millie said.

The two made their way down the stairs and out to the front porch. The porch swing was cool to the touch in the warm afternoon shade. They could see the little girls playing in the meadow from where they sat. Millie noticed that the sadness was back around Gavi's eyes as she gazed out at her little sister.

"That's why you asked if the Bible was true the same way for everyone, isn't it?" Millie said after they had sat for a while. "You were thinking about your brother and sister."

"You remember that?" Gavi asked, glancing sideways at her. She paused. "Maybe I was. Jaz has had a very hard time. And Jedidiah . . . he should have a chance to go to school. He has a good mind." They glided back and forth in silence for a time and then Gavi continued. "Grandma used to quote that verse in Jeremiah: 'For I know the plans I have for you,' declares the LORD, 'plans to prosper you and not to harm you, plans to give you hope and a future.' Gavi quoted Jeremiah 29:11 with deep emotion, then was silent again, looking down at her feet. She turned to Millie and looked her directly in the eye as she continued. "I can see how that is true for you, Millie Keith. You have so many people who love and care for you. You must wake up in the morning feeling all that love even before you open your eyes," Gavi sighed. "It's never been that way for me — for us." Gavi looked across the meadow to where Jaz was picking flowers and shook her head. "How can the Bible be true in the same way for both you and me, Millie? I just don't understand."

Lord, Millie prayed quickly. *What do I say? The fear of the LORD is the beginning of wisdom, and knowledge of the Holy One is understanding.* The Scripture God had given her on that restless night in Lansdale jumped into her mind. *Knowledge of the Holy One is understanding.*

"I don't know the answer to your question," Millie said slowly. "But I know Someone who does. I know that if you ask Jesus, He will help you understand."

"With everything that has happened . . . I just don't know if I can trust Him anymore. I may not even be able to find Him."

"I don't know what has happened in your past," Millie said carefully. "But there's another Scripture I want to share with you. It says, 'I am convinced that neither death nor life, neither angels nor demons, neither the present nor the future, nor any powers, neither height nor depth, nor anything else in creation, will be able to separate us from the love of God that is in Christ Jesus, our Lord.' Even if you feel like you have lost Him, Gavi, He hasn't lost you."

"Death nor life," Gavi said, rocking slightly, her face turned away from Millie. "Do you remember that day in front of Miss Stanhope's house? I told you that we didn't need charity." Gavi turned to Millie. "I lied. I need help," Gavi said, her brown eyes full of tears. "We need help. I don't have a single person to turn to."

Millie's Steadfast Love

"Yes, you do," Millie said, taking her hand. She hoped that the tears that welled up in Gavi's eyes meant she was beginning to trust Millie.

"I wish . . . " the young woman began, then looked away.

"What do you wish?" Millie asked gently. "I know something is hurting you, Gavi. If you would just tell me, perhaps I could help."

Gavi just shook her head. "No," she said. When she looked back at Millie, she had blinked away the tears. "Tell me about Pleasant Plains," Gavi said. "How long have you lived here?"

CHAPTER

9

Dinner Guests

God sets the lonely in families.

PSALM 68:6

Dinner Guests

*M*illie wished her parents could peek in the windows as they sat down for supper, and see the boys scrubbed from fingertips to elbows and the girls with their hair in braids and bows. Zillah had set the table with Mamma's good china for the special occasion. Gavi had insisted on helping her, filling serving dishes and arranging them on the sideboard.

Why did I ever worry? Millie thought. *Ru takes care of the animals, Zillah and Adah help with the cooking and sewing, and* (she gave a special smile to Gordon) *we have a town full of people ready to help. How can anything possibly go wrong?*

Just as Gordon was about to seat her, someone knocked at the back door. Millie opened it to find Wallace Ormsby on the porch.

"Welcome home, Millie!" he said, offering her a small bouquet of posies he had obviously picked on the way.

"Thank you," Millie smiled. "I'll put them in water and we can set them on the table. Come on in, Wallace."

"Good evening, Sheriff," Zillah said.

"Sheriff? Why, Wallace! No one told me," Millie laughed.

"What! I'm sure the news of my election as sheriff of Pleasant Plains traveled all the way to Washington! How could the newspapers in North Carolina be so remiss?" Wallace had grown into a broad-shouldered young man. His suit was of good cloth and impeccable taste, and Millie couldn't help but notice the way he smiled at her.

"Pappa says that Wallace is sure to make his mark in the world," Zillah said, taking his coat. "I think he's going to be governor at least!"

"Political aspirations, too?" Millie asked. "I never knew! Won't you join us for supper? It would be an honor to have the sheriff of Pleasant Plains at our table!"

Wallace laughed. "I must confess I am relieved at the invitation," he said. "Supper at the Keiths' has become such a tradition for me in the last year that my feet often carry me here without consulting my brain."

"He comes home with Pappa after they close the office," Adah explained.

"Well, I'm glad your feet brought you here tonight," Millie said, adding a plate to the table. Gordon came in from the kitchen and Millie was glad to see that he had removed her mother's apron. The two young men greeted each other.

"Mr. Lightcap," Wallace said as he gave the tiniest bow.

"Mr. Ormsby." Gordon bowed slightly deeper. Millie introduced Gavriel, Jed, and Jaz. When everyone was seated, Ru said grace and the meal began. Millie could not help but notice that Wallace was looking at her more than at his food. It made her feel even more uncomfortable to realize that Zillah was watching Wallace *watching her*.

"These potatoes are wonderful, Millie," Wallace said. "Light as clouds."

"I made them, thank you," Zillah said, frowning at Millie.

"Oh," Wallace said, not even glancing at her. "I never knew you could cook, Zil."

"Wallace Ormsby!" Adah said with a start. "You have been coming over for dinner for almost a year and didn't know who cooked it?"

This time Wallace did look up. "I apologize, Zillah. It's just that I'm usually so engrossed in conversation with your father that I don't notice anything at all. Your potatoes are wonderful. Did you make anything else?" He examined his plate, as if seeing the food for the first time.

"No," Zillah said. "Just the potatoes."

"I wouldn't have you think that being sheriff of Pleasant Plains is a great accomplishment," Wallace said, changing the subject abruptly and directing the comment to Millie. "I rather think that no one else wanted the job. It consists mainly of walking the streets on Friday nights and keeping watch over the taverns by the riverfront. The local people are rarely in disputes, and if they are, they take their complaints to Reverend Lord."

"I'm sure you are just being modest," Millie said.

"No, he's not," Gordon said, smiling at Wallace. "Nobody else wanted the job."

Wallace seemed to take this as a challenge and spent the remainder of the meal entertaining them with stories of life as an officer of the law. The Mikolauses ate quietly, with Gavi helping Jaz now and then. The boys seemed a little bored, as if they had heard it all before. But Zillah hung on Wallace's every word, hardly touching her food, nodding or shaking her head in sympathy. "I'm considering writing a book," he confessed at last.

"If you write it as well as you tell it, I'm sure it would be a best-seller," Zillah sighed, and looked at Wallace softly.

"Though I don't know when you'll find time to write, working in Stuart Keith's office," said Gordon, offering him a plate of biscuits.

"That reminds me," Wallace said, ignoring him completely. "I need an address at which to write your father. I haven't taken my lawyer's examination yet, and I am not fully competent to run his business without his advice."

Millie's Steadfast Love

"Pappa would not send you a letter in return — for fear the disease would be carried on the paper," Millie explained. "However, he assured me that you would do well. Have things been going well at the practice?" Millie couldn't help but think of her Pappa's promise to pay for Luke and Laylie. She had been worried by the way he guarded his funds while they traveled, and nothing she had seen at home had eased her worries.

"We will not make the money that we would have over the summer, and the winter is always slow. His absence now is not the best situation that could be hoped for."

"I have been thinking of earning money myself," Millie said. "I incurred a debt — possibly twelve hundred dollars — while in the South."

"Twelve hundred dollars!" Wallace sat back in surprise. "How could you possibly owe so much?"

"It's for the papers to free two slave children — a brother and a sister." As everyone sat quietly listening and eating, Millie gave him an abbreviated story of Luke and Laylie and how she had met them when they were on loan to Roselands during harvest time, along with their overseer, Mr. Borse. "Laylie was sent to work in the house and was assigned to be my personal slave. When she stole a medicinal ointment, I followed her to the slave quarters, where I found her brother lying beaten almost to death by Borse. I befriended them and tried to win, even buy, their freedom. When that failed, I helped them escape," Millie finished with conviction. Millie's brothers and sisters had heard most of the story from her letters, but Gavriel and Jedidiah listened with interest. When Millie finished, Wallace's head sunk into his hands.

"As a student and officer of the law, I can tell you that you have committed a serious crime," he said. "In the eyes of the law what you did was no more right than stealing a man's livestock."

"Is your picture going to be on wanted posters?" Don asked.

"Will they offer a reward for your capture?" Cyril asked, for a moment looking like he was considering turning her in.

"Are you going to arrest her?" Fan asked fearfully. When everyone looked at her, she added, "I was just wondering."

"Of course not!" Wallace said. "But this is going to have serious ramifications for Stuart. Twelve hundred dollars is a great deal of money."

"The debt is mine," Millie said. "I intend to pay it myself." Wallace simply shook his head.

"Gavi, can I have honey now?" Jaz asked.

"That's a good idea," Gavi said. Zillah went to the sideboard for the jar of honey. "We will need a butter knife," she said, taking the top off, "to spread—eeeek! A bee!" The jar flew up in the air as Zillah swung her arms like a windmill.

"No!" Cyril yelled as he dove for the jar, catching it just before it smashed on the floor. "Don't move, Zil! Stand still! The little bee's lost, that's all!" Zillah was too frightened to hear. She was busy squeaking "eeek eeek eeek!" and spinning constantly to keep her eye on the bee as it buzzed around her.

Gordon and Wallace both jumped up to help just as Zillah knocked the gravy bowl from the sideboard. Gordon tried to snatch the bee out of the air with his hand while Wallace jumped for the gravy bowl. They collided with each other, and Wallace wound up on the floor in the middle of a pool of gravy and china shards, just as the bee landed on Zillah's neck. She gave one more "eeeek!" and smacked it hard. Everyone froze. Zillah's eyes opened wide. "Ouch!" she cried. "It bit me!"

"Stung you. Bees don't bite, they sting," Cyril corrected, setting the jar of honey on the table. Millie picked it up to make sure there were no more bees.

"It hurts," said Zillah, her eyes filling with tears.

"Yeah, well think about how the bee feels," Cyril said. "You smashed it flat. If you had just stood still . . ." He shook his head in frustration, unable to find the right words to express his feelings about the loss of one of his bees.

Millie gently brushed the stinger and bee parts from Zillah's neck and applied a paste of baking soda and water to the welt that was starting to rise. Gavi and Adah cleaned up the gravy. Gordon carefully collected the broken pieces of the gravy bowl and wrapped them in a napkin. When as much order as possible had been restored, Millie served the pie, and Jaz had her bread and honey at last.

"You're not intending to hire yourself out as a domestic or shop girl are you?" Wallace asked. "Employment for ladies is very limited in Pleasant Plains."

"I don't think so," Millie said. "I won't have the time with my responsibilities here. I have been considering the matter, however, and I think I could give piano lessons. Thank you, Adah," Millie said, as her sister placed a piece of pie in front of her.

"Unfortunately, you have no piano," Wallace said. "A simpler solution might be marriage. A reasonably well-off husband—"

"A piano seems to me to be much less difficult than finding a husband," Millie said quickly. Her mind flew to Charles Landreth, who was rich enough to buy her ten pianos if she wanted them. She felt her face grow hot as everyone looked at her. "Besides, I'm not ready for marriage."

"Don't be so sure," Wallace laughed. "Anyone who can bake an apple pie like this is ready for marriage," he declared, holding a forkful aloft. "It's perfect!"

"Why, thank you, Wallace," Gordon said, batting his eyelashes. "My pie-making skills are impressive, but I am not ready for marriage yet either!"

This time Wallace blushed. "*You* made the pie?"

"And Zillah made the potatoes," Adah said pointedly.

"Did you cook *any* of this supper, Millie?" Wallace asked.

"No," Millie said, trying to hide her smile.

"It's a shame to let a perfect pie baker escape," Wallace said, joining in the laughter. "I do have a sister, Gordon. Of course she's only ten years old. But in eight years—"

"I may come calling," Gordon said seriously. "Rest assured I will bring a pie if I do. Of course, I didn't do all this cooking for nothing. I think someone promised me the story of a stagecoach ride?"

Millie and Gavi looked at each other. "I don't think I have the energy to tell it just now," Millie said.

Jed was bouncing up and down in his seat. "You were there, weren't you, Jed?" Gordon turned to him and asked. "I'll pay a nickel for that story," said Gordon.

Jed looked from Gavi to Millie hopefully. Gavi nodded and Millie shrugged.

"Wait here," said Jedidiah. He ran to his room and brought back the pages he had been working on in the stagecoach. "I wrote it down, just like it happened, so I wouldn't forget." He made quite a production of the entire thing, standing on his chair, brandishing his papers, and acting out the most dramatic moments. Fan and Annis were big-eyed, and even Cyril whistled through his teeth when Jed finished the story.

"Can he read that in Sunday school?" Don said. " 'Cause if I try to tell it, no one is going to believe a word I say."

"Forget Sunday school!" Cyril said excitedly. "We can make a fortune reading it at the dry goods store." Jed looked at him curiously. "I mean *you* can make a fortune," Cyril added quickly.

"No, he can't!" Millie and Gavriel said together, remembering Jed's soapbox theatrics.

"If I never hear about it again, it will be too soon," said Millie emphatically.

"I agree," Gavriel said, giving her brother a stern look.

"But I earned a nickel this time, right?" Jed asked, looking at Gordon.

"Well, let's see." Gordon searched his pockets carefully. "Hmmm. Nothing here. Have you looked under your plate?"

Jed lifted his plate. A shiny new nickel lay on the table under it. "Hey!" Jed snatched it up. "How'd you do that?" There was a scramble as the smaller children looked under their plates, but no one else had a nickel.

Wallace stood up. "Millie Keith, I must say you host the most interesting dinner parties I have ever attended! Unfortunately, I have to make my rounds." Zillah ran to get his coat and hat. He said his good-byes, and Millie couldn't help but notice that her sister stood watching Wallace out the window as he went down the walk.

"I think I had better be going too," Gordon said. "Rhoda Jane will be sorry that she missed this. When word gets out what entertaining dinners you host, you could sell tickets!"

Millie walked him to the front door while the girls started clearing the table.

"Speaking of selling tickets, how did you know which plate to put that nickel under?" she asked.

He pulled on his cap. "I am a keen observer of human nature," he said, winking. "All I had to do was figure out who would tell the story I had been promised. People are no harder to figure out than muskrats or mules."

"Really?" Millie said, crossing her arms.

"Take yourself," he leaned close. "You fell in love in the South, Millie Keith."

"Gordon, how did you . . . ?" Millie followed him onto the porch. "Wait! Rhoda Jane could have told you that!"

"Could have, but she didn't. And nobody needs to tell me what it means that you're here and he is not." Gordon looked across the river where the sun was sinking behind the hills like a burnished copper coin. "If he breaks your heart, you just remember—there's almost nothing I can't fix."

"He can't break it, Gordon," Millie said. "Bruise it per-haps, but not break it. My heart belongs to Jesus."

"Mine, too," Gordon said, smiling. "Mine, too," he laughed. "I have to say, though, that it's occasionally taken a pounding." He pulled his cap on and went down the steps.

Millie watched him disappear out of sight before she went inside, her own heart hurting for him. Gordon had been in love with Claudina Chetwood, and Claudina had thought she loved him too, until his hand was crippled in the musket misfire accident. It had taken Claudina nearly a year to be able to face him again, even in church. During the time she couldn't face him, Gordon had cared for Claudina's family, doing their cooking and washing when they were all sick with the ague. Gordon Lightcap simply had one of the best hearts of any young man Millie knew. *Why couldn't I have fallen in love with him instead of Charles? It would all have been so simple.*

Millie's somber mood didn't lift even after she had prepared the children for bed, listened as they said their prayers, and tucked them in. Jasmine chose to stay with her sister in the guest room, much to Fan's and Annis's dismay. They retired early, leaving Millie to talk with Zillah and Adah in the parlor.

"We're going to have to start the fall sewing as soon as possible," Millie told her sisters. "I know you have helped Mamma before, and we want to have as much of it done as possible when she gets home."

"Aunt Wealthy sent fabric," Adah said. "A whole boxful. And patterns, too. They came just before Mamma got the letter from Aunt Wealthy telling about the sickness in Lansdale. We were altering some of my old dresses for Fan. It's too bad Don and Cyril came in the middle. Hand-me-downs work so much better between Fan and Annis. Can we start tonight?"

"I don't think I could hold a needle steady tonight," Millie said. "It has been a very long day. I'm ready for bed."

"Millie?" Zillah said, tugging at the hem of her sleeve. "Will you teach me to dance? I mean, the way they do at Roselands?"

"Of course," Millie said. "But why? We have very few formal dances in Pleasant Plains."

"We *had* very few," Adah said excitedly. "Mrs. Grange decided that we should have more. Lu is having a ball, a real ball, in two weeks."

"I probably won't go," Zillah said. "I looked through all the fabric Aunt Wealthy sent and there was not one piece suitable for a gown. Nothing but calicos and rough wool."

"I have a feeling we'll be able to work something out, Zil," Millie said, thinking of her trunkful of gowns from Roselands. Zillah was just an inch shorter, but hemming was a simple task.

"You do!" Zillah said excitedly. Then her face clouded. "And . . . what do you think of Wallace?"

Millie knew Zillah was trying to be casual, but there was a little edge of worry in her voice. "I think," Millie said carefully, "that Wallace Ormsby is an excellent young man. I know that Pappa respects him."

"Do you think he's handsome?" asked Zillah earnestly.

"He is very nice looking," Millie admitted. "And now I think it's time for us to go to sleep."

When her sisters were in bed at last, Millie took her Bible and crept back downstairs to curl up in Pappa's parlor chair. It smelled slightly of her father's masculine scent. She smiled and opened her Bible to the book of Ruth, but couldn't concentrate, so she leaned back and closed her eyes for a moment. *Thank You so much, dear Lord Jesus, for bringing me home safely. I'm so very grateful to be here in this loving home with my wonderful brothers and sisters, sitting in my Pappa's favorite chair.* Millie let out a sigh of gratitude. Soon her thoughts drifted to Ruth and the hardships of life that Ruth faced. *Ruth knew what it meant to be away from her home, too. Yet I can't help but think of Gavi. Ruth had no one to care for her, either. And she had her mother-in-law to take care of. But God had a plan. Ruth became a great-grandmother to King David!*

Lord, Millie prayed, *please show Gavi what wonderful plans You have created just for her.*

Millie's Steadfast Love

Millie finally shut her Bible and stretched. It was time for bed. She damped the parlor lamp and went to the kitchen to shut the window. Night-visiting insects in the kitchen had been a problem before. She started to slide the window down, then stopped. Was that smoke she smelled? She was sure it was. Sweet, pungent smoke. She leaned out of the window to see where the smell was coming from. Someone was sitting on the porch, feet propped up, smoking a cigar. *Has Wallace come back?* Millie wondered.

The end of the cigar glowed brightly as the smoker inhaled, lighting a face. "Cyril Keith!" Millie called down in shock, almost falling out of the window. "What on earth are you doing?"

CHAPTER

10

Healing Hands

Yet, O LORD, you are our Father.
We are the clay, you are the
potter; we are all the work
of your hand.

ISAIAH 64:8

Healing Hands

*D*id your eyeballs get weak?" Cyril asked. "Can't you see I'm smokin' a see-gar?"

"I can see that all right. You wait right there, do you understand?" Millie shut the window and went out the front door. She sat down by Cyril, and Bob thumped his tail at her. Cyril took the cigar out of his mouth and examined the glowing end carefully.

"I thought you were in bed already," he said.

"I thought *you* were in bed," said Millie indignantly. "Does Pappa know you smoke?"

"Nope," Cyril shrugged. "Guess he will now, though. I was just a little too tired to head behind the wood pile — which is where I usually go." He crushed out the cigar on the wooden rail of the porch. "Too bad. I paid ten cents for this see-gar."

Millie held out her hand and Cyril dropped the horrid thing in it. "Do you believe in black sheep, Millie?" he asked, leaning back beside Bob.

"Whatever do you mean, Cyril?" asked Millie, puzzled.

"Well, didn't you ever notice that I'm different from the rest of you? I *want* to do good things, but when I try, it don't work out," Cyril said, shaking his head and staring at the ground.

"I don't think that's true," assured Millie earnestly.

"Yes, it is. If Don had given Jaz honey, do you think a bee would have crept in? I was sure I'd gotten every one of 'em out."

"I didn't see it either," Millie said, knowing that didn't really make him feel any better.

137

"Mamma's heart's gonna break just like that gravy bowl," he said. "And Pappa's not gonna be too happy about my see-gars neither. I'd think I was adopted if it weren't for that mug on Don. He's a Keith through and through, and there's no denying it. So I must be one too." He sighed and stood up. "Good night, Millie. Sorry if I spoiled your welcome home." He walked across the porch toward the door.

"Oh, Cyril," Millie called after him, "please wait." He turned back. "You didn't spoil my welcome home. But no more cigars until Pappa gets home to discuss it, okay?" Millie said, not really asking, but telling him.

"I figured you were gonna say that," muttered Cyril.

"Promise me?" Millie asked respectfully. She wanted to leave the ultimate choice up to him.

There was a long pause. "I promise," Cyril said at last.

After the door shut behind him and Bob, Millie put her hands to her face. *Was it just six hours ago that I had wished Mamma could see how well we were managing without them? Now I wish with all my heart that Mamma and Pappa were here at home to help me sort things out with wisdom.*

❧

The little Keiths were none too happy to find themselves walking to Dr. Chetwood's office the next morning. Dr. Chetwood's bedside manner was abrupt, and he was positively frightening to children. Fan dragged her feet so much that Millie had to take her hand and urge her to keep up. When Millie had explained that they could pay the doctor over time with milk and eggs, Gavi agreed to have her brother and sister vaccinated as well.

Friends and well-wishers stopped them often, welcoming Millie home and assuring her that they would be at the potluck that evening.

The doctor's office was attached to the Chetwood home and Claudina greeted them at the door. "Hello, Millie dearest!" she said as she gave her a quick hug. "Gordon says that you certainly know how to throw a dinner party. Should I have hurt feelings? You didn't invite me."

"It wasn't really a party, Claudina," Millie explained. "We somehow ended up gathering together because Gordon brought my new friends home in his wagon. And you are *always* welcome, you know that." Millie turned to introduce Gavriel, Jasmine, and Jedidiah. "We have come to see your father this morning to get smallpox vaccinations." Claudina led them through the house to the room that served as Dr. Chetwood's office. The doctor was at his desk reading a medical journal. He looked up in surprise at the invasion of grim-faced children.

"Mildred Keith!" he said, standing up. "I heard that you had returned. How are your lungs?"

Millie assured him that they were stronger than ever, and then explained her Pappa's instructions.

"An excellent idea," Dr. Chetwood said when she finished. "I would recommend every child in town who has not had the pox, and the adults as well, receive the vaccines. There have been outbreaks in Chicago and New York. And now in Lansdale, you say?" He shook his head. "It's only a matter of time before it appears in Pleasant Plains. Vaccination is so simple, but people don't trust it." He stood and opened a cabinet full of bottles and vials.

Annis's eyes grew wide as Dr. Chetwood set out a scalpel, cotton balls, and a small vial of liquid. "What's he going to do with that knife, Millie?" Annis asked.

"I will make several small cuts on your arm," Dr. Chetwood explained before Millie could open her mouth. "And then rub this liquid into it."

"Variolation?" Ru asked in astonishment. "Won't we all become ill?"

Dr. Chetwood raised his eyebrows. "Where did you learn that term?"

"I have some books on medicine," Ru said, flushing. "They're a little old."

"Reading medical books, are you?" Dr. Chetwood looked Ru up and down. Millie flushed slightly, thinking she should have made the children wear their Sunday best. Ru had come straight from his morning chores, as his overalls clearly showed. "What does your father think of that?" asked the doctor.

"Pappa approves totally," Ru said. "He has no problem with science, Dr. Chetwood. He simply believes God created it. Science can never prove or disprove God. It can only describe His creation." Millie was surprised at Ru's boldness. After Fan's terrible accident, Dr. Chetwood had done all he could for the little girl, but had told the Keiths it was hopeless—that she would surely die. After she recovered completely, the topic of science and religion became a frequent point of friendly contention between Dr. Chetwood and Stuart Keith.

"I believe I've heard your father say that before," Dr. Chetwood said dryly. "What are rubefacients?" he asked, turning suddenly to Ru.

Ru looked him in the eye. "Rubefacients excite the vessels of the skin and increase its heat. You can tell if they are working because they produce redness."

"Carminatives?" Dr. Chetwood snapped as if he were giving an exam.

"Are used for flatulency of the stomach and bowels," Ru said in response.

Dr. Chetwood nodded. "And what do your books say about variolation?"

Ru looked as if he'd passed a test only to be asked to recite his lesson, but he cleared his throat and began. "The word *variola* means rash in Latin. That's where variolation comes from. Scabs from people with smallpox are gathered and ground to a powder. You can rub it into a wound or inhale it. If you have a patient with smallpox, you can use pus from a sore and introduce that into a wound."

"And this keeps them from developing the disease?" Millie asked, more than a little impressed by her brother.

"Not at all!" Dr. Chetwood said. "The variolated patient does develop smallpox, but a much milder case. A process that was very helpful to General Washington's troops in 1778. But modern science marches on. We have a much better method now. The modern procedure is vaccination. It comes from the Latin word *vaca*, for cow." He picked up the small bottle he had set out earlier. "This vial contains material from the udder of a cow infected with cowpox. It is a *miracle* of modern science." He glanced at Ru, as if demanding a reply.

"Isn't it incredible," Millie said, stepping up beside her brother, "that though creation has fallen, God has given us minds to find such solutions and hearts that reach out to poor sufferers?"

Dr. Chetwood harumphed at her and turned back to the table. "However it came about, once I rub this into a wound, you will never get smallpox. Not even a mild case." He picked up the scalpel. "Now roll up your sleeves. You will want the vaccination high on your arm where the scar won't show."

The smaller children backed up against Millie. Adah looked at her in panic. "You're not going to let him cut us, are you, Millie?"

"Come, come," Dr. Chetwood said. "It is completely safe. You will experience only a moment of pain."

Ru started to roll his sleeve up, but Millie stepped forward. "As the oldest," she said, "I will go first."

"Excellent!" Dr. Chetwood indicated the chair and Millie sat down. She rolled up her sleeve and looked the other way as he made three crisscross cuts with the scalpel. She had to bite her lip to keep from crying out as tears came to her eyes.

Dr. Chetwood did not seem to notice her grimace, but went on with his work. "This is the finest vaccine available," he said as he moistened a piece of cotton with the liquid from the vial and pressed it into the wound. "It came all the way from London, from the Royal Academy, where they raise and infect cows to produce it." He bound the cotton in place with a bandage, then turned to Ru, who rolled up his sleeve and sat down.

"Did it hurt, Millie?" Don whispered.

"Yes," Millie said. "But not unbearably. I'm sure you're as brave as I am, Don."

Ru watched the doctor slice open his arm with interest, and even helped apply the vaccine. Don sat down next, his chin held high, almost defying the doctor to make him cry. But just before the scalpel touched his flesh, he said, "Wait! Can I have a musket ball?"

"A musket ball?" Dr. Chetwood said.

"The mountain men bite musket balls when they have to have an arrow cut out," Fan explained.

"How about a piece of cotton?" the doctor asked.

Don frowned. "Mountain men don't bite cotton."

"Very well." Dr. Chetwood rang a bell and the butler appeared. "Bring me a musket ball from the case in the hall." Don gripped it between his teeth as the doctor picked up the scalpel once again and made the three cuts.

Don rubbed the musket ball dry on his shirt and passed it to Cyril, who clamped it between his teeth. He made a manly groaning noise with the first cut, and sucked the air in through his teeth with the second; but with the third he was silent.

"There," Dr. Chetwood said when the bandage was in place. He held out his hand for Cyril to spit the lead slug into. Cyril pursed his lips, but nothing came out.

"Come on, young man, spit it out," Dr. Chetwood said.

"Can't." Cyril shook his head. "I swallowed it."

"And what would your mountain men do now?" Dr. Chetwood asked Fan.

"That never happens in the books," Fan said. "Is Cyril going to die?"

"Yes," Dr. Chetwood said grimly. "But not for sixty to eighty years, I hope."

"Then can I get a musket ball too?" asked Fan, climbing into the chair.

"Certainly not!" Dr. Chetwood said. "I would have to raise my fees to pay for them all."

Millie had to hold Annis in her lap and hide Annis's head on her shoulder while Ru held her tiny arm steady for the doctor. Gavi, Jed, and Jaz were last. Afterwards, Jaz sobbed and ran to her elephant, Cyril, who picked her up and hugged her, glaring at the doctor as he held her close.

"All finished," Dr. Chetwood said with satisfaction. "You will develop scabs on the vaccination site, but you are now completely safe from the smallpox. No swimming until the scabs fall off. And Rupert? You may read in my library any time." Ru thanked him and picked Annis up, then they departed.

"Ru, I had no idea you knew so much about the practice of medicine," Millie said as they walked up the street. "I thought all you were interested in was steam engines and machines."

"The body is an amazing machine," Ru said, "designed by God Himself. Our muscles and bones are like pulleys and levers and our heart like a pump. All of the parts must be in good working order."

"I think you would make a marvelous doctor," said Millie, smiling at him.

Ru shrugged. "I would have to go to school, and that takes money." He swung Annis up onto his shoulders and started walking. Millie watched him as he walked, more determined than ever to find a way to earn money.

Annis was tired and fussy all the way home, and Millie was happy to lay her down for a nap. She was very grateful that she did not have to prepare dinner that night, as her arm had begun to ache and all of the children were cross. Annis and Jaz were far too little to understand why they had been hurt. Jaz had bumped her arm on the way home, and now Gavriel held Jaz on her lap in Marcia's rocking chair as the little girl cried herself to sleep. Millie's arm hurt too, but she tried to occupy herself by helping Adah with the smock she was shortening to fit Annis.

"Gordon's a little early for the potluck," Adah said, looking out the window. Gordon was coming up the walk swinging a basket. Adah hurried to open the door.

"Hey, Gordon!" called Don, coming up behind him eagerly. "Has Rhoda Jane been making cookies?" Don said hopefully.

"She has," Gordon said. "But you will have to wait until after supper. Do you have a pint of milk?" he asked as Millie came up behind Adah in the doorway. "And six or seven eggs?"

"You hungry?" Don asked him. "We've got some pie left over."

"We *had* some pie left over," Ru corrected him, appearing behind Millie. "You'll have to settle for eggs and milk," said Ru, looking at Gordon.

"I'm not here to eat," Gordon said. "I am here to prove that there's nothing that's broken that cannot be mended." He looked at Millie. "Do you have the pieces of your mother's gravy bowl?" he asked.

"They are in the kitchen," Millie said.

Gavi pulled a knee warmer over Jaz and they all followed Gordon to the kitchen. He took a bottle of vinegar, a box of quicklime, a sieve, and a small camel's hair paintbrush out of the basket. Don and Jedidiah fetched a pint of milk and half a dozen eggs from the well-house while Millie brought out the pieces of the bowl neatly wrapped in a napkin.

Gordon spread the broken pieces out on the table, fitting them together like a puzzle. When he was sure he knew where each piece fit, he poured the pint of milk in another bowl and added the vinegar. The milk instantly curdled into white lumpy curds and yellowish whey. He poured the whey into a different bowl. "Bob might like these curds," he told Fan, carefully handing her the bowl. Fan carried them to the porch for the dog and hurried back to watch. Gordon added the whites of the eggs and then started beating the mixture. Finally, he had Cyril sift the quicklime through the sieve, while he mixed until he had a paste. "That should do it," Gordon said. He used the paintbrush to coat the broken edges of the gravy bowl with the mixture. He began fitting them neatly together, working quickly, even with his crippled hand. As the gravy bowl became larger, he had problems gripping it.

"Let me help," Gavi said, taking it from him. They both bent down close over the table, working intently to put the bowl back together. Don nudged Millie and pointed at them, puckering up his lips as if he were kissing. Millie frowned at him. When the bowl was done, with even the smallest pieces back in place, Gordon took it carefully from Gavi and held it up.

"There you go, Millie!" he said. "Almost as good as new—and it won't come apart, not ever."

"Where did you learn to do that?" Gavi asked.

"My father was a stage actor," Gordon said. "And a very good one, too," he winked. "That means, of course, that he had to do odd jobs to keep his family fed—smithing, tinkering, mending, and occasionally making patent medicines. He was really good at a lot of things." He picked up his basket then, smiling. "Another thing he taught me was when to make an exit," he said, walking to the door. "I'll be back with Rhoda Jane and the girls tonight," he said.

Millie tried to go back to her sewing, but her heart wasn't in it. "I think I would like to take a walk," she said to Gavi, "if you are going to be here to keep an eye on the children?"

"I'll be here," Gavi assured her.

Millie went to her room for her sturdy walking shoes and a wide-brimmed bonnet. As she left the house, she took a

deep breath and sighed. *It's so good to be home again.* Joy welled up inside her, and her steps quickened. She found herself practically running down the hill to the bridge. She crossed the stream and then ducked through the thick underbrush by the road until she found a deer trail that led into the marsh.

The Kankakee was stirring with life. The birds were making a joyful noise from every tree and bush. It seemed as if a pail of musical notes had been tossed into the air to spill around Millie along with the sunshine. Millie added her whistle to the symphony, but the birds—harsh critics that they were—refused to sing along and remained silent until she stopped.

Millie was careful to pause every now and then and look at her surroundings, and to look back the way she had come to memorize the trail—a trick Gordon had taught her when she first came to the marsh. The watercourses and the game trails were ever-changing, so it was easy to become lost, even in a place you had been many times before.

Millie had thought of the wildness and wonder of the Kankakee many times during her stay at Roselands. The swamps and bayous in Louisiana had been similar, full of life, but they had been missing something, and until this very moment, Millie had not known what it was. The sky. They didn't have the marvelous blue Indiana sky stretched above them. Millie spread her arms and turned her face up.

She carefully made her way to the deep pool where she had watched a muskrat just days before leaving for Roselands. How long ago that was! She was surprised to find a huge beaver dam rising out of the water. "Civilization!" she said aloud to the marsh.

Millie's Steadfast Love

The willow tree she had so often rested against had beaver tooth marks on the bark, and the huge old giant had become an ambitious project for a beaver. Millie settled herself in the roots and leaning against the tree, she spent an hour talking to Jesus about Charles, Aunt Wealthy, Cyril, her Mamma and Pappa, and Gavriel. The more Millie thought about it, the more sure she was that the young woman had been on the verge of telling her some secret that afternoon on the porch. There was something broken inside of Gavi, and the sharp edges hurt her heart. *But there's nothing broken that can't be fixed. Surely if Gordon Lightcap could work wonders on a gravy bowl, Lord Jesus, You can work miracles in Gavi's heart. Only You will use love and understanding instead of milk and eggs. Was it simple chance that placed Gavi and Jaz and Jed on the same stagecoach as me and Pappa, Lord? Or was it what Aunt Wealthy would call a divine appointment? You see the sparrow when it falls,* Millie prayed. *I know You see the tears in Gavi's heart, and You know why she cries.* Millie prayed until she ran out of words, then sat quietly for a long time amazed by the detail of God's creation, until an emotion too large to describe filled her heart and mind. She felt her body tingle all the way to her toes. Millie was filled with awe as she felt the presence of God all around her. *Is this the fear of the Lord?* she wondered. Somehow she was sure it was.

On her way home, Millie met Claudina and Bill Chetwood and Lu and Teddy Grange coming up the hill.

"We came a little early for the potluck!" Claudina said, indicating the basket Bill was carrying. "We are going to have such a feast! Celestia Ann and Rhoda Jane arranged it all. I'm surprised we're not having an official 'Welcome-Home-Millie-Keith' parade!"

"You should have come on the Fourth of July!" Teddy said. "We would have shot the cannon off an extra time and carried you through town."

"Don't be ridiculous!" Millie laughed. "I should be throwing an 'I-Missed-My-Friends-So-Much' party! You can't imagine how wonderful it is to be back in Pleasant Plains!" Millie practically skipped the rest of the way home.

"Hey, Bill!" Don called from the yard as they approached. Don started toward the garden gate, but Cyril jumped over the fence and beat him to it, pulling it open with a flourish and waving the guests through. "What's in the basket?" Cyril asked. "Wait! Don't tell me." He closed his eyes and breathed in. "Fried chicken!"

"You're right as rain," Bill said, "but that's not all."

Cyril put his hand up. "I'm not done. Fried chicken and corn muffins!"

"You have a nose like an—"

"Elllllllephant!" called Jaz, standing on the front porch with Fan, who was clapping her hands.

"Who's she talking about?" Teddy asked.

"Nobody," Cyril said quickly.

"Yes, it's you," said Fan, frowning at him. "You said you would be her best elephant!"

"You're an *elephant*?" Teddy crowed. He made a show of examining Cyril's profile. "You do kinda have a trunk for a nose!"

"He's not just an elephant," Bill pointed out. "He's her *best* elephant!"

Millie could see Cyril's fingers curling into a fist.

CHAPTER

11

True Confessions

*Let's have a feast
and celebrate.*

LUKE 15:23

True Confessions

$\mathscr{H}$elp me take the chicken inside, Cyril," Millie said quickly. She grabbed the basket in one hand and her brother's arm with the other and pulled him up the steps into the house.

"Jaz didn't mean any harm," Millie said, as soon as they were alone.

"It's not Jaz I'm thinkin' about," Cyril said. "Fan didn't have to say I was the best elephant. She knows Bill and Teddy like to make fun of me. I'd like to—*pow*!" He jabbed his fist like a boxer.

"Cyril! You will do no such thing! Bill and Teddy are our guests," Millie scolded.

"How do you know I wasn't talking about Fan?" he asked.

"Because you are a gentleman," Millie said. "And gentlemen never hit ladies. They think of another way to express their feelings."

"Like how?"

"Well, you could—" Millie began.

"Is everything all right in here?" Rhoda Jane asked as she and Gordon came into the kitchen carrying baskets and boxes. Celestia Ann and Reverend Lord were right behind them.

"Everything is fine," Millie said, giving Cyril a look. "Let's not talk about it now, Cyril."

"But Millie, I . . . "

She raised her eyebrow the way Mamma did when a discussion was over. Cyril shrugged his shoulders and walked away. Millie didn't have time to follow him because it suddenly seemed the whole town was trooping through the

153

Keith kitchen. Most of the ladies not only brought a deli-cious-looking dish for the meal, but "a little something" for the pantry, too. Millie found herself very busy making sure everyone was accommodated; finding enough plates and napkins became quite a task as more and more friends arrived. Another knock at the front door brought Millie hurrying from the kitchen after making sure all the new-comers had what they needed. She opened the door to find herself confronted with the entire membership of the Pleasant Plains Ladies Society.

"What do you think you're doing, Millie Keith?" Mrs. Prior asked, her fists planted firmly on her hips. "You give me those napkins right now and you sit down." Mrs. Prescott pulled a chair onto the shady side of the porch and Mrs. Chetwood motioned to it.

"Marcia Keith would not approve of your working so hard—I'm sure of it," Mrs. Prescott said. "You are just back from your convalescence."

"I'm in perfect health," Millie protested.

"She looks a little pale," Damaris Ransquate said, eyeing her closely.

"I think she looks flushed," said Mrs. Prescott, who could never agree with Mrs. Ransquate. The two women eyed each other over Millie's head.

"I am fine, I assure you," said Millie. She started to get up, but Mrs. Prior put a restraining hand on her arm. "Now, now," the woman said in her no-nonsense-from-you-young-lady voice. "Your mother wasn't planning on being away for more than two weeks when she left. She must be worrying her head off over you all. I think we should split the children up." She looked around at the other ladies, who nodded. "Your brothers and sisters could go back to the families who were caring for them before you returned. You can stay here and get plenty of rest."

"Pappa told me to bring the children home with me once I got back to Pleasant Plains. And Mamma said not to let the boys misbehave." Millie suddenly felt as if she was twelve years old again and had to fold her hands to keep from reaching up to see if she were wearing pigtails. Celestia Ann opened the front door and joined the group of ladies on the front porch. Millie shot her a "Help me!" look and they both smiled.

"You do seem to be fully recovered," Mrs. Monocker said.

"Yes! That's what I have been telling you!" Millie said with relief. "I am quite well —"

"But these things can be deceiving," Mrs. Monocker continued, "like an Indian summer. They seem to be gone and then they come back with a terrible vengeance. I don't know what your mother was thinking, sending you to take care of the household all alone."

"Ladies! Ladies! Millie appears well enough," Dr. Chetwood announced, approaching the group of ladies on the porch. Mrs. Prescott threw a look at Damaris Ransquate. "Roses in her cheeks and a twinkle in her eye!" he said. "Has your cough recurred?" he asked Millie.

"No," Millie replied to the doctor. "Thankfully, it has not. I feel stronger than I have ever felt before."

"It is a scientific fact," Dr. Chetwood said, "that certain constitutions are better suited for milder climates. Others can only thrive in the cold. Lives can be changed by changing location."

"My trip to the South certainly did that," Millie agreed.

"The doctor says that she is fine," said Celestia Ann, speaking up for the first time. "And I am sure Mr. and Mrs. Keith considered everything you have mentioned before they gave Millie the responsibility." Millie looked gratefully at her friend.

"I, for one, am willing to help carry Millie's load in any way possible," said Mrs. Ransquate. The ladies looked at one another.

"Well, what are we waiting for?" Mrs. Prescott asked.

Before Millie knew what was happening, her life was ordered and arranged by the ladies of Pleasant Plains. Mrs. Grange and Celestia Ann were to be in charge of cooking; Mrs. Chetwood and Mrs. Prior would stop by twice a week to help with cleaning. "And I'll come by Mondays and help with laundry," Mrs. Roe said. "Beth likes to help me, and we'll just make a day of it!"

"Thank you all," Millie managed meekly.

Just then, Cyril wormed his way through the crowd of ladies, Fan in tow. The elephant had apparently lost his princess. He stopped a few feet from Dr. Chetwood and pushed the little girl forward. "Go ahead, ask him," he said, pushing his sister forward.

Fan's mouth opened, but no words came out.

"Speak up, child!" Dr. Chetwood commanded. "There's nothing wrong with questions!"

"Did you say vaccination was from . . . c-c . . . cows?" Fan stammered.

"Correct. From cowpox, a disease which —"

Cyril grabbed her arm. "Thanks, Dr. Chetwood," he said, dragging her away.

"You certainly have a curious family," the doctor said.

"By curious, do you mean that they ask questions or that they behave in a questionable way?" Millie asked.

The doctor raised his eyebrows. "Both, now that I think of it."

"Now, Doctor, the Keiths are decent folk," Mrs. Roe said. "This town is better for them."

"Of course we are, of course we are," Dr. Chetwood said. "I certainly didn't mean to imply anything different."

Millie grabbed Gavriel, who was just passing by on her way back to the kitchen. "I believe you have met Gavriel, Dr. Chetwood," she said. "But I'm not sure I have introduced her to everyone here." Millie made the introductions, and Gavi smiled and nodded at each woman, repeating their name. "I'm pleased to meet you all," said Gavi, then she excused herself and went back to helping Rhoda Jane serve.

Mrs. Monocker sniffed. "I don't want to question the friends you keep," she said. "But where did these people come from? I never heard your parents speak of any relations named Mikolaus. That's a peculiar, foreign-sounding name."

"I'm sure I do have foreign relations," Millie said. "And I expect some of them even have peculiar names, but the Mikolauses are new friends."

"Let's get busy, ladies," Mrs. Prior said. "We have people to feed!"

They set about seating people on blankets on the lawn and chairs on the porch and directing Ru and Gordon to set up tables with sawhorse legs and wooden tops for the food. When everyone was eating, Helen stood and tapped her teacup with a spoon until she had everyone's attention.

"I have heard rumors of a most exciting story," she said, looking from Millie to Gavriel.

"Oh, no," Millie said, covering her face. "Not again."

"Come on, Millie," Nicholas shouted. "Don't be shy. We want to hear the story of your adventure!"

Millie's Steadfast Love

Jed was summoned once again and the porch became his podium. All of Pleasant Plains seemed to stare gape-mouthed first at Millie and then at Gavi as he read. It was such a success that after he finished, he put his papers down, weighted them with a rock so they wouldn't blow away, and called on Cyril, Fan, and Don to help act out the more dramatic moments. Cyril insisted on playing the part of Fenris Jones, while Jed played Gavi and Fan played Millie.

Gordon leaned against the tree beside Millie, who was wishing she could disappear.

"I have decided that it's not true," he said as he watched the budding actors.

"What do you mean?" Millie said.

"I think that boy writes fiction, not fact. Take the very first thing—Gavriel looking like a boy. Who would believe that?" He turned to pick up Jaz, and Millie saw Gavi's face just behind him. The girl had a glass of cider in each hand, which she had obviously been bringing to Millie and Gordon, but she stood frozen in place, blushing to the tips of her ears. Then she turned and walked quickly away without a word.

After the meal, the older folks said their good-byes, promising to pray for Aunt Wealthy, Stuart, and Marcia.

"A household is not a runaway stagecoach, Millie Keith," Mrs. Prior said on her way out. "It is a good deal more difficult to control than a few stampeding horses. If you have any trouble at all, you just call on me!"

Gavi stood on the porch beside her as Millie waved farewell to her guests.

"The next time," Gavi said through gritted teeth that looked almost like a smile, "let's just let the stagecoach fly over the cliff. Our lives will be shorter, but much less embarrassing." Millie could only chuckle in agreement.

There was enough flour, salt, ham, cheeses, canned fruit, and vegetables left on the table to assure Millie that she would not have to restock the pantry before her parents returned. Millie's friends stayed to help clean and put things away.

"You haven't said a word about the parties," Claudina said. "Were the young men dashing?"

Millie thought instantly of Charles Landreth and Otis Lochneer. "Yes . . . and no," she laughed. "They did have excellent manners. They could dance and sing . . ."

"I can dance and sing!" Gordon said. "Would you like to hear?"

"No!" Wallace and Bill chorused. Everyone laughed.

"What kind of gowns did they wear?" Helen asked.

"Young men don't wear gowns," Fan informed her, which caused everyone to laugh again.

"I did have many gowns made," Millie said. "Perhaps I can show you another time," she offered, glancing at Wallace, Gordon, and Bill.

"Or perhaps these boys can just sit down here while we look at them," Helen said with her usual grace and charm.

"No need," Gordon assured her. "I, for one, have work to do." Bill and Wallace followed his cue.

"Gavi," Jed said as the young men were leaving, "did you pick up my story? I thought I left it on the porch, but it's gone."

"One of the ladies must have picked it up," Millie said. "There were so many people helping clean up."

Ru offered to take the Princess Jaz and her ladies-in-waiting, Fan and Annis, down to ride the horses while he worked in the barn, and Millie found herself in her room surrounded by her sisters and friends.

Claudina gasped when she saw Millie's gowns of satin and silk. "Did you ever imagine this?"

Millie smiled at her friends, wishing she could share her dresses with every one of them, as they had shared with her when she left for Roselands. If it hadn't been for their generous gifts of clothing, she would have gone looking like a rag doll.

"I would love to borrow this one!" Claudina said, glancing at Millie's trim figure. "I don't see why you couldn't have put on some weight while you were away. Did you have dress balls every night?" Claudina twirled around the room, holding the gown next to her and making the skirt swish. "Candlelight dinners, music . . . did you break any hearts, Millie?"

Millie felt herself flushing and turned away, but not before Helen noticed.

"Millie Keith! Did *you* fall in love?" the older girl asked, fixing her eyes on Millie with a keen gaze.

"I . . . " *Why hide the truth?* thought Millie. *It's no secret at Roselands that Charles proposed to me.* She felt her cheeks grow even brighter.

"Mind your own beeswax!" Rhoda Jane said, putting her arm around Millie's shoulder.

"No, it's all right, Rhoda Jane. Really. I definitely did not fall in love. I was dragged into it kicking and screaming. It has been the most unpleasant experience of my life."

"Not really!" Claudina said, collapsing onto the bed. "I can't believe you would ever fall in love."

"Claudina!" Lu said.

Claudina looked around. "What I meant was, Millie is so sensible. Sensible girls do not have romances."

"It wasn't that Charles you wrote about, was it?" Lu asked. "What is he like?"

Millie found herself totally at a loss for words. How could she describe Charles? It wasn't his smile or even the twinkle in his eyes that she loved; it was his heart.

"Was he rich?" Helen asked.

"Well, yes," Millie said reluctantly. "And good-hearted. Charles is the kind of man who would treat a little slave girl like a princess, and a princess like his sister."

"And did he treat you like a sister?" Helen asked.

"Of course not!"

"*Really?*" Helen's eyebrows arched. "Tell us more!"

"Leave her alone, Helen," Rhoda Jane said. "Can't you see she has a broken heart?"

"It's not really broken," Millie said with a sigh. "Charles Landreth asked me to marry him." There was silence in the room as this sank in. "Three times," Millie added ruefully.

"He is handsome, rich, good-hearted, *and* he asked you to marry him *three times*?" Claudina was fanning herself with a hat. "Millie!"

"I said no," Millie said with a finality that she did not feel at the moment. Claudina gasped.

"Claudina, will you please try to be less dramatic?" Rhoda Jane said. "Millie had a perfectly good reason — the best reason, really."

"Charles is not a Christian," Millie explained. "I pray for him every day. And even though I would love all of you to pray for him too, it does hurt to talk about it."

"So let's not talk about it," Rhoda Jane said, and all the girls looked at her. "Are you going to wear this one to the ball, Millie?"

Millie's Steadfast Love

"No," Millie said. "I believe Zillah's going to wear that one."

Zillah gasped. "Really? I am?" she cried with delight.

"I do believe it is the most suitable," Millie said. "And it will be simple to hem."

The talk went back to dresses and hats, but one by one, the girls said their good-byes and started home before the sun went down.

Millie gathered the children together to listen while Ru read from the big family Bible in the parlor. Afterwards, Millie tucked the little ones in with kisses and hugs, and listened while they said their prayers.

"Millie?" Fan asked as Millie was leaving the room. "Do cows dream?"

"I think so," Millie said.

"What do they dream about?"

"Well . . . I believe Bobforshort dreams of chasing rabbits," Millie said with a smile. "Haven't you ever seen his feet twitch or heard him wuff in his sleep?"

"Yes," Fan said.

"So maybe cows dream of acres and acres of sweet clover. Good night now, Fan."

"Good night, Millie."

Millie went to her own room and sat down to write her mother and father a letter. She was sure her mother would be relieved to hear of all the help they had been offered. She considered telling them about Cyril's cigar smoking, thinking long and hard about whether to mention it in a letter, and finally decided not to. He had promised not to smoke again until they returned, and it would only worry them.

CHAPTER

12

News from New York

*As it is written, "How beautiful
are the feet of those who
bring good news!"*

ROMANS 10:15

*D*on, would you carry this letter to the post office?" Millie asked when the lessons were done the next morning. She would have loved to take the letter herself, but she knew that Mrs. Prior would be by any moment to help with the housework. Millie was determined that there be nothing left to do when Mrs. Prior arrived. She had already set Zillah to stripping the bedding, and Fan and Annis were gathering fresh flowers for the parlor and the dining table, while Gavriel cleaned windows and dusted sills.

"Can I finish my chapter first?" Don asked. "I just have two pages to go . . . "

"I'll do it!" Cyril said jumping up. "I'll go."

"Thank you, Cyril," Millie said, handing him the letter. He snatched it from her hand and dashed upstairs. It wasn't until she heard the front door slam behind him that she wondered why he had gone upstairs before he left. He couldn't have been getting money for cigars. He'd promised. She decided to talk to him when he came home, just in case.

Millie went to work rolling up rugs to be hung and beaten. Zillah helped her carry the heavy rolls to the backyard. She had just hung the first rug when Mrs. Prior appeared.

"It's a fine day for beating rugs," she said approvingly. "Sunny and bright. We should get through these in no time."

Millie took the heavy wooden paddle and swung it hard. Dust and sand puffed from the rug when she hit it. Because of the sandy soil in Pleasant Plains, rugs had to be beaten frequently, but it was not Millie's favorite job. She was wiping her brow by the time Mrs. Prior offered to take the paddle. They rolled each rug when it was beaten clean and stacked it on the back porch. When the last rug was rolled, they swept, mopped, and dusted the whole house before carrying the rugs back inside.

Millie rubbed the palms of her hands. The rug-beating paddle and the broom had raised a blister on her hand, and her shoulders ached. *I forgot how much work keeping house is. How did I ever imagine I could have it all finished before Mrs. Prior arrived? How will I ever get it done at all?*

"A woman's work is never done," Mrs. Prior said, seeming to echo her thoughts. "But there comes a time when you must set it aside for the next day. I'm ready for a cup of tea." Millie put the teapot on the stove and found a plate of cookies. It was wonderful just to sit down.

"I think you girls are doing fine here," Mrs. Prior said as she finished her tea. "Your mother would be proud. I will be going now, but Mrs. Lord will be here tomorrow and you can do your baking then. Mrs. Chetwood will come the day after."

Millie picked up the flowers from the table. "Thank you," she said. "Won't you take these home to your family tonight?"

As soon as Mrs. Prior had gone, Millie and Gavriel set about making dinner. "I've told you before that I am not very good in the kitchen," Gavriel said. "I'm afraid that I'm about to prove it. There are so many things I should have learned from my mother while I could. But I wanted to spend my time with the horses. Now I have to make a home for Jed and Jaz, and I don't think horse sense will help me."

"Cooking is simple," Millie assured her. "You just have to learn a few rules and how to follow a recipe."

"How about a trade?" Gavi said. "I will teach you what I know about horses and you teach me what you know about kitchens."

"It's a deal!" Millie said. "You can make the mashed potatoes tonight. They are easy." She showed Gavi how to peel the potatoes, taking the thinnest sliver of skin so there would be no waste. Gavi was starting her fourth potato when Millie saw Cyril out the window.

"Keep peeling. I'll be right back," Millie said. She hurried out the front door and caught her brother before he came inside.

"Millie, there's a . . . " began Cyril.

"I need to talk to you, Cyril," she said, before he could finish. "You aren't up to something, are you?"

His eyes opened wide. "What would I be up to?"

"I was just thinking that you might be tempted, going by the dry goods store."

"You think I went to town to buy a seegar?" He looked hurt. "I promised I wouldn't, didn't I? All I did was go to the post office . . . an' I didn't read your letter, either, 'cause it was all folded up!"

"I'm sorry," Millie said. "I shouldn't have accused you of anything."

Cyril just looked at her with a hurtful look in his eyes, saying nothing. Then he stalked away.

The kitchen had gotten crowded while Millie was away. Zillah was helping Gavi peel potatoes, while Fan and Adah had dressed Jaz and Annis in princess gowns made of pillow slips with pins in the corners. Don and Jed had helped themselves to the rest of the cookies on the plate and were dipping them in a teacup full of milk. Millie found enough space to slice ham for frying.

Cyril wandered in and perched himself on the kitchen stool with his whittling knife and a piece of pine.

"Find anything at the post office?" Don asked.

"Yes," Cyril said. "There was a package for Millie."

"A package!" Millie stopped in mid-chop. "Why didn't you tell me?"

"Started to," Cyril shrugged, still looking hurt.

"I'm sorry that I didn't listen to you. Where was it from?"

"New York City," Cyril said. "They want one dollar postage."

Millie pulled down the tin where Mamma kept her milk and egg money, and shook it. It was empty.

"I will have to wait until Pappa returns," she said, putting the tin back on the shelf.

"That's weeks!" Adah said. "I can't wait that long! Did you see it, Cyril? How big is it?"

Cyril pursed his lips. " 'Bout this big." He measured ten inches with his hands.

"You have the money, Cyril," Zillah said. "You *always* have money. Why don't you pick up the box for Millie?"

"I'm afraid it will just have to wait," Millie said.

"Guess so," Cyril said, concentrating on his whittling.

Don winked at Millie and wiggled his eyebrows up and down.

"I'm glad he's not picking it up," he said. "Seems to me the only people Millie knows in New York are those peculiar ones she met down South. No telling what they could be sending her. It could be a warning that she's a fugitive from the law, or a warning that sheriffs are onto her where-abouts."

Cyril's knife stopped, the wood shaving curled around the blade. "Think so?" He considered that for a moment, and then went back to whittling. "Naw. Why send a box for that? A letter would do."

"Anybody can read a letter," Don pointed out. "What if they are offering a reward, like Fan said? Now a box is tied up with paper and string. You can't just open it up and read what's inside."

"Yeah, Cyril," Adah said. "Anyone can read a letter."

Cyril whittled on in silence, while Don fished broken cookie bits from his milk.

"You think I should pay for that box?" Cyril asked at last.

"Nope," Don said, leaning back. "I like it better where it is, sitting on a shelf, full of mystery and promise. There could be anything in that box, anything at all, and that's the way I like it."

"All right," Cyril said, putting his knife down. "You convinced me. I'll pay the price. Do you want to go with me?"

When the boys returned carrying the parcel, everyone crowded around Millie. Cyril offered his pocketknife, and Millie cut the strings, then carefully pulled off the paper.

"Take the lid off," Cyril said anxiously, about ready to burst.

Millie lifted the lid to reveal a beautiful brown rag doll, dressed in a forest green cloak and cap. It had button eyes and a sweet red smile.

"It's Laylie," Millie laughed, holding it up for everyone to see. "She's safe in New York!" Millie softly fingered the cape. While at Roselands, Laylie had imagined herself as the outlaw of Sherwood Forest, and the little children of the slaves' quarters had been her Merry Men. Millie had cut up her own green gown to make the slave girl a Robin Hood cloak for Christmas. "Thank You, Lord, that she's safe," Millie prayed out loud, closing her eyes for a moment in gratitude.

"It's a doll?" Cyril said in disgust. "I paid a dollar for a doll?"

"That's not all," Zillah pulled a paper from the bottom of the box. "There's a letter, too."

It was from Miz Opal, the woman who had smuggled Luke onto a ship bound for New York in a coffin, with Laylie dressed as a mourner by her side. Millie began reading the letter out loud:

Dear Miss Keith,

I know you must be wondering and worrying and praying about your young friends. Rest assured, they arrived safely in New York City, though the first leg of our journey was a trial. The captain of the ship was a Southern sympathizer, so Luke had to stay in the coffin, save for brief moments when we could be sure no one was watching. Laylie spent the whole trip sitting on top of it, reading the Bible aloud, and Luke couldn't do anything but lie there and listen through the air holes. She read the Gospels first, and then the story of Jonah in the belly of the whale. And every morning and every night she read Psalm 116:

> *The cords of death entangled me,*
> *the anguish of the grave came upon me;*

News from New York

I was overcome by trouble and sorrow.
Then I called on the name of the LORD:
"O LORD, save me! . . .

You have freed me from my chains.
I will sacrifice a thank offering to you
and call on the name of the LORD.
I will fulfill my vows to the LORD
in the presence of all his people.

I've heard it so many times it will be with me always, but I can't help but think the words had a whole different meaning for these children who were fleeing slavery and death. It must have been terrible, being trapped inside that box so long. Jesus was only in the tomb for three days, but Luke was in the coffin for eight, with nothing to do but listen to his sister read the Bible, and think.

Millie shuddered at the thought of Luke being locked in a small, dark box that long. She took a deep breath and continued reading:

We carried the coffin off the ship at Philadelphia and through the streets on a cart until we reached the home of a member of the Friends Church, and Luke was quiet the whole way. When we opened it at last, the smell was terrible, but Luke wouldn't get out.

He had such a look on his face that I was afraid he had gone mad. Laylie started crying, but Luke asked for the minister to pray with him, and kneeling inside that coffin he asked for the forgiveness of his sins, and he forgave those who had beaten him. Luke asked Jesus to be his Savior and Lord! Everyone was crying when he stepped out of that coffin, come from death to life. "I couldn't get out before I got rid of those sins," he explained. "I didn't want to bring them with me out of the grave. They can stay in the death box where they belong!"

Luke makes Laylie read the Bible to him day and night. He said he has no mind for learning to read, so he is memorizing the book of John, word for word, line for line, verse for verse. When he has it memorized, he is going to go back. Like Jonah, he is sure he is sent to the people he once hated. Luke is going to preach the Gospel to Borse.

"Isn't Borse the overseer who beat him?" Zillah asked. "Isn't that what you wrote to Mamma?"

"Yes." Millie realized there were tears running down her face. "Borse beat him half to death. Borse is the man who killed Luke's mother."

"But . . . won't Borse kill him, too?" Ru's face was pale.

"God won't let that happen," Adah said. "Not if Luke is following God. Right, Millie?"

"I don't know," Millie said slowly. "They killed Jesus. And they killed the apostle Paul for preaching about Jesus, and all of the other apostles, too, except John."

"But . . . Borse is an evil man," Adah said. "Why would God waste Luke's life on him?"

"Jesus would never ask us to do something He hasn't done Himself." Millie was sure of that. "But Jesus did die for Borse," Millie said. It was the only answer she could think of. "Jesus must have wanted him to be something other than an evil man. How can Borse know that, if someone doesn't go and tell him?"

"What else does the letter say?" Fan asked.

Millie started reading again.

News from New York

The trip from Philadelphia to New York was more pleasant. Laylie traveled as my niece, and Luke as the Colonel's manservant. Unfortunately, Isabel Dinsmore offered a huge reward — two thousand dollars — for their return. The flyer reached New York before we did, though how it happened I cannot say. We are in a race against time. Luke will go back, slave or free. Pray that God gives him grace to memorize the Scriptures before he is captured, so that he can complete his mission before he is killed.

Pray that our precious Savior will keep Laylie safe. They both want me to tell you thank you, Millie Keith. Thank you for helping them escape and especially for telling them about Jesus.

A servant of His, Opal

"Two thousand dollars," Millie said, lowering the letter. "That's so much!"

"What does it matter now?" Zillah asked. "He is going back."

"If Luke dies," Millie said, wiping away her tears, "I want him to die a free man."

CHAPTER

A Date With Jesus

May the Lord direct your hearts into God's love and Christ's perseverance.

2 THESSALONIANS 3:5

A Date With Jesus

hat's that smell?" Ru asked.

"My potatoes!" Gavi wailed, rushing to the stove. The water had boiled off and smoke was pouring from the pot.

Millie grabbed a towel to wrap around the pot handle, and then carried it outside while the boys opened the kitchen windows and Zillah and Adah fanned the smoke out. Millie attempted to rescue the potatoes by scraping the unburned portions into a bowl, managing to leave most of the burnt portions in the pan.

"Use a fork to mash them," Millie said, handing the bowl to Gavriel. "Then just mix in butter and milk and a little salt to taste."

Millie could not stop praying for Luke and Laylie as she set the scorched pot on the stove to boil with soda water. *If twelve hundred dollars is impossible, how will I ever earn two thousand? Our house on Keith Hill cost only a little more than that.*

Ways to earn money were discussed and discarded over dinner. "I've got two dollars and sixty-two cents," Cyril said, fishing in his pocket. He pulled it out and dropped it on the table. "It's yours, Millie."

"What good is that going to do?" Jed asked. "That's nowhere near what she needs."

"It's what I've got." Cyril glared at him. "I'd give more if I had it."

"Thank you, Cyril." Millie took the coins and put them in the money tin. "It's more than I had before, and it's a good start."

The dishes were passed around the table, and Ru picked up the mashed potatoes. "These look good," he said, scooping up a big dollop on the serving spoon. Millie watched in horror as a gray-white cord stretched up from the bowl when he tried to lift the spoon. He lifted it higher, and the cord stretched like a rubber band before snapping back into the bowl. Ru grimaced as he tried to shake the potatoes off the spoon onto his plate. They weren't shakable.

"Hey!" Fan said. "People buy glue!"

Every eye turned to Gavi, who looked back at them solemnly for one moment, and then burst into laughter. It was the first time Millie had heard her laugh, and soon the whole table was giggling with her. It changed the whole mood of their evening, and they were still telling potato-glue jokes even later while Millie helped Zillah and Adah with the alterations on their dresses for the party.

It wasn't until Millie was finally able to sit down with her Bible that Luke and Laylie returned to her mind. *Impossible*, she said to herself.

What does Jesus think of that word? Surely it says something about that word in the New Testament. She looked it up in her concordance. There were only five instances of the word *impossible* in the Gospels, and she looked up each one, starting with Matthew 17:20.

"I tell you the truth, if you have faith as small as a mustard seed, you can say to this mountain, 'Move from here to there' and it will move. Nothing will be impossible for you." Then she read "Jesus looked at them and said, 'With man this is impossible, but with God all things are possible.'" She looked up one more reference in the book of Acts: "But God raised him from the dead, freeing him from the agony of death, because it was impossible for death to keep its hold on him." By the time Millie had read the verse in Acts, she was laughing out loud. *The word impossible means nothing to Jesus!* Millie realized with awe.

"Does reading the Bible make you feel better, Millie?" Fan had crept up to her and was looking earnestly into her sister's face.

"Yes," Millie said. "Much better."

"Who is King Neb . . . Nebubula-sneezer in the Bible?" asked Fan, crinkling up her nose to try and pronounce the big word.

"There is a Nebuchadnezzar," Millie said with a smile. "Is that close enough? He was a king in the time of Daniel the prophet."

"Will you find it for me?" asked Fan.

Millie turned to the book of Daniel. "Would you like me to read it to you?" Millie asked. "It's not very long."

"No," Fan said. "I want to read it myself." She pulled Millie's Bible up on her knees and started reading. She was still holding the Bible when Millie finished saying prayers with the boys, but she was staring into space.

"Did it make you feel better?" Millie asked.

Fan just shook her head. "My tummy hurts," she said. Millie got her a cup of warm milk and then carried her up to bed. "Does your tummy still hurt, Fan?" Millie asked as she pulled the light coverlet up to the little girl's neck.

"Yes," Fan said. "Do I look all right, Millie? I don't look . . . different, do I?"

"Of course you don't," Millie said, smoothing her sister's hair. "Why would you think such a thing?"

"Oh, no reason," Fan said, but her lip trembled.

"Are you sure you don't want to talk about it?"

"No," Fan said. "I don't want to."

After Fan was in bed, Millie read through the first four chapters of the book of Daniel, trying to find what had upset Fan. But she closed the Bible no more enlightened about Fan's strange behavior than she had been when she opened it.

~~~

The household quickly fell into a routine. The boys helped Ru with the animals while Millie and the older girls cooked breakfast. They ate the morning meal together, and then Ru went to work on his gardens in the cool of the morning, while Millie and Gavriel listened to the smaller children read their lessons. Millie soon found that Gavi was very good with the younger children. She had a quiet, loving heart, but it troubled Millie that when she talked about the future or the past, it was Jed and Jaz she spoke about, never herself. The younger Mikolauses settled into the house as if they had been born there, but Gavi's eyes were always going to the road, and then the sad and haunted look would return. Millie prayed for her daily, but Gavriel showed no desire to talk about it.

Every day at noon, one of the members of the Pleasant Plains Ladies Society would arrive to help with cooking or housekeeping duties. When they were done, the children were allowed to play in the gardens or at the foot of the hill. Their vaccination scabs had not fallen off so swimming was forbidden, but Millie took them on walks to town or down the hill to the Lords' cottage behind the church.

Celestia Ann was happily arranging for the baby who was "coming to visit" in September by turning Reverend Lord's small office into a nursery. The young couple would walk back up Keith Hill with their visitors to have dinner, Reverend Lord bringing along a book to read aloud after the meal. With the help of a reluctant Ru, or

Gordon if he happened to be visiting, Millie and Celestia Ann gave Adah and Zillah dance lessons for an hour each evening in preparation for the Grange ball. Everyone seemed to be happy in their routine except Fan. The little girl grew quieter by the day. Even playing princess with Jaz did not cheer her up.

"I don't know what to do with her," Millie confessed to Rhoda Jane and Gordon one afternoon as they sat on the porch with Gavi watching the little girls play. "She seems so moody, and she hasn't been 'wondering' about anything at all. Do you think she could be missing Mamma?"

"Perhaps she needs a distraction," Gavi said. "What does she like to do?"

"She loves the horses," Millie said, "especially Inspiration. But I can't let her go riding alone, and I have no time to go with her."

"There's plenty she can do with them right here," Gavi said, standing up. "Fan!" Fan looked up from her play at the sound of Gavi's voice. "Would you like to help me teach Inspiration to talk?" Gavi called out.

"Horses can talk?" Fan asked, skipping toward Gavi.

"I think I need a distraction too," Gordon said, looking after Gavi. Rhoda Jane rolled her eyes at Millie, and they all walked to the pasture.

"Inspiration is a very smart horse," Gavi said. "She is always polite, and does what she is told. That means she is ready to learn new tricks."

"Glory tries to kick," Fan said.

Gavi nodded. "Glory is not ready to learn tricks. May I borrow a hat pin, Millie?" Millie took a pearl-headed pin from her straw bonnet. "And I will need some carrots, if Ru can spare them from his garden."

Fan ran to ask and soon came back with a bunch of freshly pulled carrots. Gavi shook the dirt from them, broke one into four pieces, and put them in her apron pocket. She tied a lead rope to Inspiration's halter, then tied her loosely to the top rail of the fence.

"Now you are going to learn a trick," the girl said. Inspiration's ears pricked toward Gavi. Gavi put the hat pin between the fingers of her right hand, with the sharp end pointing out.

"Don't stick Inspiration with a pin!" Fan cried. "That's not nice!"

"I'm not going to hurt her," Gavi said. "I'm just going to touch her with it. She will think it's a fly and shake her head to get rid of it."

She took the lead rope in her left hand. "Are you a mule?" she asked, and patted her right hand just above Inspiration's withers. The mare shook her head.

"Good girl!" Gavi said instantly, and pulled a piece of carrot from her pocket.

"The trick to training a horse," she explained, "is finding something the horse was *made* to do—like chase away flies—and teaching them to do it on command."

"I knew that," Gordon said. Rhoda Jane gave him a look. "I did!" he insisted.

Gavi asked Inspiration the same question again, and again touched her lightly with the pin. When the horse shook her head, Gavi praised her and gave her a piece of carrot. She repeated this six or seven times, then said, "That's enough for one day. Will you help me again tomorrow, Fan?"

Fan helped her every day, and within a week, Inspiration would shake her head "no" when Fan asked her if she was a mule, and nod her head "yes" when Fan asked her if Jaz was a princess.

Gordon, Emmaretta, and Min were the first audience for Fan's horse show.

"You're wonderful!" Gordon said proudly. He clapped for Fan and Inspiration, but his eyes went to Gavriel.

On the day of the Grange ball, Adah and Zillah began to prepare for the party at noon. Millie could only smile, remembering her first dress ball and how she, Annabeth, Bea, and Camilla had fussed over their dresses and hair.

"Can I use Mamma's combs, Millie?" asked Zillah, turning from side to side to make her skirts swish.

"I don't think Mamma would approve of you wearing your hair up just yet," Millie said, surveying Zillah in the rose-colored gown. Her sister was growing into a beauty. Millie wished there were some way to save the picture for her mother, to keep it trapped in a mirror. Marcia would be sad to have missed their first ball, but Millie knew it would break the girls' hearts to stay home.

"But Millie, this gown is too sophisticated for a bow in my hair!" Zillah pleaded. "I'll look like an infant! Helen says—"

"Helen can take it up with Mamma when she comes home," said Millie. Then seeing the disappointment in her sister's face, she added, "I'll help you curl your hair with an iron. It will be beautiful with a plain ribbon, and I'm sure Mamma would approve."

"Mine, too, Millie?" Adah asked hopefully.

"Not yet," Millie laughed. "You are only twelve." Adah sighed, but she was far too excited at being invited to the dance to argue much about her hair.

Millie's Steadfast Love

Millie waited until her sisters were dressed before she put on her own gown, a lovely sea-green dress with simple lines and no lace. She twisted her golden hair into a French knot, but out of consideration for Zillah she did not wear Mamma's ivory combs herself.

"Promise you won't stand by us," Zillah said when Millie appeared.

"Why ever not?" Millie asked, surprised.

"Because no one will dance with us if you do," Adah explained. "You are too pretty."

"Nonsense!" Millie said with a smile. "I'm just older, that's all. I'm sure you will have plenty of partners."

When Mrs. Prior, who had insisted on watching the younger children, arrived, Gavi, Ru, Millie, Adah, and Zillah started down the hill. Gavi had been convinced to go to the ball only with great difficulty. She wore a dark red dress, and the effect of it with her black hair and eyes was lovely. The twilight was enough to see by, but Ru carried a lantern and pole for the return trip home. Adah stopped every few feet to practice her dance steps. Zillah caught her breath as the sounds of a string quartet drifted toward them on the soft evening air. "Listen, Millie!" Zillah said. "Have you ever heard anything so beautiful?" Young people in carriages, wagons, and on horseback called and waved as they went past. Many, Millie knew, were from nearby towns. Some had traveled all day to get to the ball. They would change into their party attire, dance the night away, and sleep at the homes of friends or relatives.

The Grange's house was the most substantial building in town—a red brick mansion with white columns supporting the porch and wide well-kept lawns and gardens on the grounds. A large paved patio had been cleared for dancing,

184

and the quartet sat on the porch in between the wide columns. A full moon rising above the trees bathed the scene in pearly light, adding a touch of enchantment. Lu, dressed in a silver gown that shimmered like the moonlight, was greeting guests as they arrived. "What do you think, Millie?" she asked. "The theme of the evening is Shakespeare's Midsummer Night. Have you ever seen anything like it?"

Millie looked out across the crowd. Some ladies wore satins and silks, but many were in calico and cotton. Some young men wore suits, and others homespun and boiled white shirts. But they were all talking and laughing. There was something comforting about the social mix of the Indiana frontier. In the South, the social lines were clearly drawn, and you would never see the poor at a party with the rich like you saw here. Even the matrons of the Pleasant Plains Ladies Society, sitting in a formidable row along the dance floor's edge and watching over the dancers, made Millie smile. "I have never seen anything like it," Millie said truthfully. "It's wonderful, Lu."

They made their way to the corner of the patio. Zillah's eyes were searching the crowd and Millie was certain she was looking for a certain tall, handsome sheriff. Millie smiled and waved at Gordon and Rhoda Jane. Suddenly Zillah made a strange squeaking noise, and Adah clapped her hand over her sister's mouth. Wallace Ormsby had appeared, waltzing with a young lady Millie did not recognize.

"Can we go stand over there?" Adah asked, taking Zillah's hand comfortingly.

"I'll go with them," Ru offered. Millie noticed that he led his sisters quite close to the refreshment table, where he could help himself.

"Hello, Millie, Gavi," Gordon said, walking up. "Would you care to dance?" He held out his hand toward Gavi, but she had already turned toward a seat under a tree and apparently didn't see it.

"Yes," said Millie, quickly putting her hand in Gordon's to spare him any embarrassment. Wallace spun past with his partner as they began to dance. Millie nodded, but he quickly turned away.

"What's wrong with Wallace?" Millie said.

"The same thing that ails us all," Gordon sighed. "Millie Keith has broken his heart. Woe, woe . . . "

Millie stepped on his toe none too gently.

" . . . wouch! Did you learn that step in Charleston?" he asked lightheartedly.

"That and a few others," Millie laughed. "You know I have never broken your heart, Gordon Lightcap!"

"That's true," Gordon said with a smile. "I was only a hopeful, never an intended."

"Will you do me a favor?" Millie asked, looking up at him earnestly.

"Of course," he said.

"Dance with Zillah and Adah at least once tonight."

"I'm not sure I can whisk them from under the gaze of the Ladies Society," he laughed. "They are not going to let any harm come to Marcia Keith's children while she is away. And dancing with a Lightcap! It could start rumors."

"You misjudge yourself," Millie said. "Every one of those ladies knows you have a noble heart. I'm truly thankful for them," Millie said. "I'm sure I couldn't run the house without them. We are very well taken care of."

"In that case," Gordon smiled as he spoke, "I will dance with each and every one of those ladies, in your honor!"

"You will dance with every lady here tonight because you love dancing. Admit it!" she teased.

"What's true is true," Gordon laughed back at her. "What's wrong with Gavriel?" Millie followed his glance and saw Gavi sitting alone in the shadows.

"I think she's shy. She doesn't really know any of the young men here."

"She knows me," Gordon said. "Do you think that I could convince her to dance?"

"If anyone can, it would be you."

The music stopped and Gordon bowed to Millie, then he started toward Gavi. However, it seemed she would not be convinced, as Gordon ended up dancing with Beth Roe.

Millie accepted two more dances and then stood back to watch as Gordon escorted first Adah and then Zillah to the floor. Zillah may have danced with Gordon, but her eyes were on Wallace the whole time.

I wish Mamma would come home, Millie thought. *I can hardly rule my own heart, and I have no idea what to say to my sister. But I do know how she feels. All of the young ladies at Isabel's parties had wanted to be Charles's partner. He's probably dancing with one of them somewhere tonight. Does he remember me? Does he ever think about me?* Millie shook her head. *Give me wisdom, Lord,* she prayed, *and strength.*

Millie walked a little farther from the dancers, and when she was sure no one was watching, she curtsied low. *Will You be my escort tonight, Lord? There are some things I would love to talk to You about.* She started down the garden path. *Let's start with the moonlight. Don't You think You made it a little too romantic?* she sighed. *Of course You don't. You looked at the moon You made and said it was good. You created love, so that must mean You created romance, too.*

Millie's Steadfast Love

She stood still, looking up at the sky. *The same silver moon must be shining down over Roselands, over Charles, over Luke and Laylie far away in New York. Shining down over all the good and evil in the world. I know I can't love someone more than You do. You, Heavenly Father, loved us enough to send Your only Son to die for us. Was it hard? Harder than my giving up Charles? It must have been, because You knew what they would do to Your dear Son. I don't know the end of the story with Charles. Would it be harder if I did?*

She walked again, through patterns of moonlight and shadow on the ground. *Are You going to send Luke to die? Let him die a free man, Lord. Nothing is impossible for You.* Millie stopped. "Since nothing is impossible for You, would You send me two thousand dollars?" she asked aloud. The amount was so huge that Millie had a hard time saying it. "So that Luke and Laylie can be really and legally free. And while we are on the subject, I would really like a miracle for Charles. For me and for Charles," she corrected. "I want to marry him, Lord. You know I will follow You first and always, but You must admit, You made something wonderful when You made him. I can only imagine how much more wonderful he will be when he is the man of God You created him to be. Help him to know You."

Millie walked in the gardens until eleven o'clock and then started back to the party. She paused just outside the circle of light, watching the happy guests laugh and talk. Ru, Zillah, and Adah were standing by the refreshment table again under the watchful eyes of the Ladies Society. Wallace was dancing with Helen, but Millie was surprised to see Gordon on the bench talking to Gavriel. His head leaned toward her, and Millie suddenly remembered the kiss-faces Don had made when Gavi had helped to mend the gravy bowl, and Gavi's blush when Gordon said she could never look like a boy. Millie smiled. *Maybe Gordon's heart wasn't destined to be broken forever. Romance was God's idea, after all.*

Ru had worked his way from one end of the refreshment table to the other several times, and he was only too glad to leave the party, but Adah and Zillah wanted to stay.

"Wallace hasn't asked her to dance yet," Adah whispered to Millie.

"It's very late and I'm sure Mrs. Prior would like to go home to her own bed," Millie said. Ru led the way with his lantern pole even though the moon was bright. Millie linked her arm with Zillah's and let the others walk ahead.

"I would like to tell you something Mamma told me once," said Millie. "It's about giving your heart to Jesus."

Answered Prayers

I will search for the lost and bring back the strays. I will bind up the injured and strengthen the weak.

EZEKIEL 34:16

ordon Lightcap found the most surprising reasons to visit Keith Hill during the next few days. Things needed mending that Millie had not known were broken. Emmaretta and Min insisted on visiting with Fan every single day, and Rhoda Jane volunteered to help Gavi learn to cook. Gavi was perfectly happy to listen to Millie talk for hours about Charles or her adventures in the South, but whenever Gordon's name came up, Gavi blushed and changed the subject. She sat quietly during his visits, and Millie was sure she was trying not to call attention to herself. As soon as he was gone Gavi became herself again, working hard at learning to cook and spending many hours in the kitchen with Celestia Ann and Reverend Lord, who were over almost as often as Gordon.

"Is something wrong with you, Celestia Ann?" Fan asked the former housekeeper one afternoon as Millie sat in the kitchen, her needlework in her lap. "You look fat."

"Nothing's wrong with me," Celestia Ann assured her with a laugh. "Is something wrong with *you*? You look thin." Celestia Ann felt Fan's brow for a fever. "Would you like to help us make bread?"

"No," the little girl said. "I'm going to go see my new best friend."

"Who's her new best friend?" Reverend Lord asked as Fan wandered away.

"Belle," Adah said.

Millie's needle stopped in mid-air. "Belle the cow is Fan's new best friend?"

Millie's Steadfast Love

Adah shrugged. Millie decided that she would have to have a talk with her sister as soon as the Lords were gone. Then the conversation turned to abolition. Reverend Lord asked if Millie had changed her views in any way since visiting the South.

"They have only grown firmer," Millie said. "I think that slavery is more cruel and horrible now that I have seen it firsthand. Before it was just words on a page. I believed what I read, but that is nothing compared to coming face-to-face with it. Now I have seen the bloody backs and heard the piteous cries of the sufferers. I have also seen the courage of the Christian slaves."

Reverend Lord nodded. "I'm afraid much of my flock experiences the Bible in the same way you once knew slavery. They read the words in the book, but they have never come face-to-face with the living God. They behave as if Jesus were just a historical figure and all that is required of them is living a good life—which they are perfectly willing to do, so long as it does not interfere with their comfort. They visit in God's parlor once a week and feel that is enough of His company."

"But isn't living a good life enough?" Gavi asked. "Following the Ten Commandments?"

"What do you mean by good?" Reverend Lord said. "It seems to me that *every* Christian should be able to say with Paul the Apostle, 'follow me as I follow Christ.' We should be setting an example for the world."

Millie snipped the end of her thread. *Should I dare ask anyone to follow my example? I am trying to follow Jesus with all of my heart and I still make mistakes.* "But what if you're not perfect?" Millie asked. "How can you expect to lead anyone?"

"That was Paul's very thought," Reverend Lord said with a smile. "In Philippians 3:12, Paul said, 'Not that I have already obtained all this, or have already been made perfect, but I press on to take hold of that for which Christ Jesus took hold of me.' Paul knew he was not perfect. But it's not called a walk of faith for nothing. A walk has a beginning and an end. And there are troubles along the way—at least there were for the great apostle. His life was a great adventure!"

"Speaking of adventures," Celestia Ann said, "I've had enough for one day."

"Follow me," Reverend Lord said, holding out his hand and escorting his wife to the door. "Oh! Millie!" he said as he turned back, pulling a letter from his pocket. "I almost forgot. Mrs. Monocker mentioned that she had received this in yesterday's post and I happened to have the amount necessary for postage, so I brought it along for you."

Millie felt a chill when she saw the handwriting on the letter. *Charles!*

"Thank you," she said, putting it in her apron pocket. Millie watched through the window as they started down the walk, Celestia Ann leaning on her husband's arm and laughing up at him.

She tried to focus on her stitches, but after she stabbed her finger the third time she gave up. Lace collars would be no use to Annis with blood all over them.

"I would like to take a little walk," Millie said, "if you don't mind watching the children, Gavi."

"Of course," Gavi said. "I will be right here. Take as long as you like."

Millie practically ran down the steps and around the house to her swing. She pulled the letter from her pocket and unfolded it with shaking hands.

Millie's Steadfast Love

Dearest, Dearest Millie,

Ha! I can just imagine your face as you read that greeting. There's nothing you can do about my calling you that, after all. You are a thousand miles away! I troubled Mrs. Travilla for your address, as Isabel did not seem inclined to provide it. I can imagine the reason for her sudden dislike of you. I'm almost tempted to explain the circumstances to her, and perhaps she would be done with her endless matchmaking. Her new victim is a distant relation from her own side of the family, Penelope. The lovely Penelope sings and dances and has a wit every bit as sharp as a marble. I miss your lively conversation.

Millie could hear his voice in the words, and it made her tingle from her head all the way down to her toes. She continued:

You should know that you are no less troublesome at a distance of a thousand miles. I would much rather that you were here so that I could look into those big blue eyes and say, "Millie, you have mud behind your ears," or perhaps "There is spinach stuck in your teeth." You are the only young lady who has ever told my aunt that she should wear feathers like a bird. Ah, how I miss you!

I am reading your book, by the way. I started in the beginning, and though it seemed quite lively for a while, with blessings and smitings and quite a plotline, I am afraid it is weary going now. I am currently wading through the text of Leviticus. I cannot fathom the reason for all of these rules and regulations. What kind of God would require us to kill animals because we have sinned? Why does He need blood to satisfy Him? Why don't you come back and explain it to me?

Wishing I were yours forever,
Charles Landreth

Millie waltzed across the lawn and up the steps. *Charles hasn't forgotten me! And he's reading my Bible!* She took the letter to her room and hid it away in the drawer with the rose.

Returning to her sewing, Millie found it hard to focus, so she started supper early, humming to herself as she stirred the pot of soup and mixed up the dumplings.

"Where's Fan?" Millie asked when the children assembled for supper. The children looked at one another.

"She must be with Ru," Don said. "We haven't seen her since this afternoon at dinner."

"Wasn't she playing dolls with you?" Zillah asked Annis.

"No," Annis said. "Just me and princess Jaz. We made a blanket house."

"*I'm going to visit my new best friend.*" Millie suddenly remembered hearing Fan's voice. *How could I have forgotten that I was going to check on her after the Lords left?* Millie chastised herself silently.

The meal was left untouched on the table as a thorough search was made of the house, outbuildings, and barn. Belle looked at them with sad brown eyes, but if she knew where Fan was, she wasn't telling. The Keiths met again at the kitchen table.

"Could she have gone to visit Emmaretta Lightcap?" Millie asked.

"She could have," Adah said uncertainly, "but Fan never went visiting alone before. Mamma always had one of us walk with her."

"What if she is drowned!" Zillah cried. "Or stolen?"

"Don't talk nonsense," Millie said, but she felt icy needles prick her heart. Her sister was missing and she didn't even know how long she had been gone. "We are simply going to have to find her. How many friends does Fan have in town?"

"The Lightcaps," Adah said thoughtfully, "and she likes to visit with Mrs. Prior."

"She might have followed the Lords," Gavriel suggested. "She adores Celestia Ann."

"Zillah, run to the Lightcaps. Adah, go to the Lords. Boys, I want you to run into town and ask Mrs. Prior if she has seen her."

"I want Fan!" Annis said and started to cry.

Jaz's lips pressed together and she put her arms around Annis. Then she turned to Cyril. "Elephant! You must take me to Fan in a hurry." Cyril just looked pale and shook his head.

Millie turned to Annis and Jaz, kneeling down in front of them. "You two little girls are going to have to help by staying here with Gavriel," Millie said. "Just in case Fan is taking a nap somewhere close by the house. You wouldn't want her to be all alone when she woke up, would you?" The two shook their heads solemnly. "Good. Now you eat your supper, and we will be back soon." She grabbed Ru's arm and dragged him to the other room. "Check the rowboat and the riverbank," she said. "I'm sure Fan would never go there alone, but we have to be certain."

"Where are you going, Millie?" asked Ru.

"I'm not sure yet. Fan was upset this morning and I should have talked to her. She may be hiding." Millie did not want to say that she was going to check the edge of the Kankakee. The marsh was far more dangerous for a small child than the riverbank. Fan could swim like a fish, but that was no help in the miring mud or with the water moccasins or bears she might meet. All kinds of terrible pictures flashed through Millie's mind as she went to her room to pull on her walking shoes. *Jesus*, she prayed, *take care of Your little lost lamb. Help us find her. Please keep her safe!* She went down the stairs two at a time, pulled open the front door, and ran straight into Cyril. He had a rope looped around Bobforshort's neck, and Millie nearly toppled off the porch before she could untangle herself from the boy and dog.

"Cyril Keith!" Millie gasped, catching his arm to keep from falling. "Didn't you go with Don and Jed?"

"Nope," Cyril said. He nodded toward Bob. "Fan trained him to find me if she gave him a noseful of my scent. He can track her, too. He needs something to sniff, like a shoe or shirt. Are we going to stand here jawin' or are we gonna find her?"

Millie ran to Fan's room and searched for something the little girl had recently worn. Mrs. Prior had been there the day before and she was much too efficient for dirty stockings or clothes of any sort to be left lying about. Millie finally settled on the pillow Fan had slept on, pulled the slip off, and ran back downstairs.

Cyril took the pillowslip and held it under the hound's nose. "Let's go huntin', Bob!" he said, pulling the loop over Bob's head. Bob stuck his nose into the pillowslip and whuffed in a great noseful of scent, then wagged his half tail and started to sniff around the porch. He moved back and forth, nose to the boards, then let out a yelp and set off across the yard.

"He's got her," Cyril said. "Come on!" They followed the hound across the yard to the stables, where Fan had apparently stopped by Inspiration's stall before she went on to the milking barn. Here Bob snuffled all over the place, from the milk stool to the hay trough. Fan had apparently spent some time here with her new best friend Belle.

Millie's Steadfast Love

"Fan?" Millie called hopefully, thinking she might be hiding in the hayloft, but Bob's head whipped up, and with a bark he was off again, out the back door of the barn and down the path toward the back fence.

"Keep up, Millie!" Cyril called back over his shoulder. "We gotta run!" Millie lifted her skirts to her knees and followed as fast as she could. Cyril's overalls didn't slow him down at all as he scrambled over the fence, but Millie's skirts did not fare as well. Her calico caught, but she pulled it savagely and went on when it tore free. Cyril was outdistancing her, but even he had to stop for breath when they reached the bridge over the stream.

"Where's Bobforshort?" Millie gasped.

"Shhh." Cyril put his finger to his lips. "Don't breathe so loud. We've got to listen."

For some moments there was no sound at all except the babble of the stream, and then, from deep in the swamp, a bay. The marsh that Millie loved suddenly didn't seem friendly at all, not with her sister lost in it.

"He's got a trail," Cyril said. "That's either Fan or that raccoon we been chasin' all summer!" Bob was off again, with Cyril and Millie right behind him. It was harder now, as they could only follow the sounds of Bob's quest, and often had to make detours around ponds or areas too marshy to wade through. Finally, he let out a deep, long bay.

"He's got it treed," Cyril said assuredly. Millie gave him a puzzled look. "Her treed. I mean her, Millie," Cyril finished quickly.

It was perhaps a quarter mile more, much of it wading knee-deep in muck, to a small tussock covered with ancient trees. One of these had fallen, and the abbreviated end of Bob was protruding from the end of it.

"Go away, Bob!" they could hear Fan's voice echoing from inside the log. Millie sent up a silent prayer of thanks as Cyril grabbed Bob's tail and pulled him out.

"Fan?" Millie said. "Come out of there now."

"No!" Fan said. "Go away. This is my house. I'm going to live here for a long, long time."

"But aren't you hungry?" Millie asked, leaning over to peer into the darkness. "What will you eat?" There was a long silence.

"You won't have to worry about that, I guess," Fan said, in a terribly sad voice.

"Why not?" There was no answer from the log. "Please come out," Millie said.

Cyril shook his head at her. "You been away too long, Millie," he whispered, then in a louder voice, he said, "Hope you ain't been in that log mor'n a minute or two, Fan."

"Why?" Fan sniffed.

"It's full of chiggers, that's why. They're probably diggin' into you right now."

There was a mad scrambling and Fan appeared — wet, muddy, and disheveled, slapping at her arms and legs. Millie grabbed her in a hug, but the little girl went stiff in her arms.

"Let me go!" she said. Millie set her down, but kept a firm grip on her hand.

"Well, she's safe and sound. Guess Bob and me will be goin' now." Cyril was off and running before Millie could stop him, Bob hard on his heels. Millie shook her head and turned back to her sister.

"What could possibly be so terrible that you would want to run away?" Millie asked tenderly.

Fan looked up at her with tear-filled eyes. "I'm turning into a cow," she said. "That's what."

"Whatever gave you that idea?"

"Cyril said so," Fan said as she wiped her tears with grubby hands. "He said that most folks don't get sick with the cowpox vaccine, but some do. He said it turns you into a cow. The first thing you get is a rash. If you get it on your hands, you get hooves first. If you get it on your ears, then they turn into cow ears. You just wake up one morning, and there they are." Fan burst into tears.

"Fan, you don't have a rash on your hands or ears," Millie said, trying to comfort her, but Fan just sobbed harder.

"It's . . . on . . . my . . . tummy," she wailed between sobs. "That . . . means I'm going . . . to grow an . . . udder!" she stammered out finally, collapsing into Millie's arms.

"Fan, baby," Millie said, sitting on the log and pulling her onto her lap. "You are certainly not going to grow an udder. People do not turn into cows," she said, stroking Fan's head as she spoke.

"That's what I said," Fan muttered through broken sobs. "But Cyril said they did too. He said it's in the Bible. And I looked it up and read the story. King Nebuchadnezzar was a cow for seven seasons."

"Oh, my sweet, precious girl!" Millie said. "He didn't turn into a cow. He was out of his mind. He only *thought* he was a cow, so he crawled along on all fours and ate grass. Wasn't that silly of him?"

"Didn't he have cowpox?" Fan's hiccups were growing less violent.

"Of course not. Cowpox is a sickness that milkmaids get. It gives you little blisters on your hands, but that's all.

Please, Fan, let's get you home and into some dry, clean clothes. I'm not very comfortable in these wet skirts and petticoats. Are you?"

"No," Fan admitted. "Are you sure I'm not going to grow an . . ."

"I promise," Millie said with certainty. "And everybody is looking for you. We were all very worried." Millie held out her hand and Fan took it.

They hadn't gone far before Fan started dragging her feet. "Will you carry me, Millie?" Fan asked. "I walked a long time before I found my log house."

Millie pulled the little girl up onto her back. Fan's muddy petticoats quickly soaked through Millie's blouse, the only part of her that had been dry. The added weight made walking through the mud much more difficult. Millie stopped every few moments to rest. This portion of the marsh was little traveled and the ground was mushy at best, underwater at worst. Millie had been longing for a walk in the marsh, but this was not what she'd had in mind. She kept a close eye out for water moccasins, but saw only harmless snakes hunting for the mice and lizards rustling in the undergrowth they passed.

Fan seemed to grow heavier by the step. Millie finally had to set her down and rest. "I'm hungry, Millie," the little girl said.

"Well, you should not have run off before supper," Millie said. "Next time Cyril tells you such a story, you should come and ask me if it's true."

"All right," Fan agreed. Millie pulled her on her back again, and they started for home once more.

The Keiths were all waiting when Millie finally trudged up the hill. Cyril had told everyone that Fan had been

found, and apparently why she had run away, for a lovely purple shiner was blooming over his right eye.

"What happened to you?" Millie asked.

"Nothin'," Cyril said, but his eyes went accusingly to Don.

⁓

"What were Mamma and Pappa thinking, leaving me alone with the children?" Millie asked Gavi, after the little ones had been put to bed.

"Well, it's not a complete disaster," Gavi said.

Millie looked at her. "It's not?"

"Of course not. Cyril could have *two* black eyes," Gavi said with a laugh. "You can't tell me Cyril's never had a black eye before. And everyone is now safe in bed. Who could ask for more than that after such a day? Besides, you only have three more weeks before your mother and father come home."

CHAPTER

Trouble on Keith Hill

He has showed you, O man, what is good. And what does the LORD require of you? To act justly and to love mercy and to walk humbly with your God.

MICAH 6:8

Trouble on Keith Hill

Three more weeks, Millie sighed as she lay in bed the night. A little of the fear Millie had felt the night at Mrs. Hartley's crept in. *The house is in order, the cooking's done, but surely Mamma would have figured out what was troubling Fan long before she ran away. Have I spent too much time worrying about myself? About Charles?* "Give me wisdom, Lord," Millie prayed out loud. "Help me be a good example to my brothers and sisters, as Mamma has been to me."

How have Mamma and Pappa been an example to me? Before I could read, or even understand the story of Jesus, they were showing me who He was through their obedience to Him. "Follow me, as I follow Christ," they'd said. Make me obedient, Lord. I want my life to shine like that. And Lord, please reveal Yourself to Charles as he reads Your Word. Let that double-edged sword that You speak of in Hebrews 4:12 pierce his heart, his soul, his spirit, his marrow, dear Jesus. Help him learn to know and love You—not for my sake, but for Yours.

The next morning Cyril showed up for breakfast to a cold reception from Jed and Don. His dark purple eye was swollen almost shut. "Hey," he said, starting to sit by Jaz.

"No!" Jaz said, putting her little hand over his plate. "You're not my best elephant anymore! You were not nice and I don't want you!" she said emphatically.

Cyril turned on his heel and walked out. Millie caught up with him on the porch.

"How does your eye feel?" she asked.

"It hurts," Cyril shrugged. "How's a black eye supposed to feel?"

Millie's Steadfast Love

"Does the rest of you hurt too? Jaz is just a baby, but I'm sure Fan would forgive you if you said you were sorry. Sometimes . . . sometimes it helps to cry."

"Cry?" He gave her a disgusted look. "I'm not a girl. I don't cry. The whole thing was your fault anyway."

"My fault?" Millie felt her temper starting to rise. *Lord, give me wisdom!*

"You're the one who said I couldn't hit a girl. You said to find some other way to work it out."

"I certainly didn't mean lying to your sister," Millie said. "You have been making some very bad choices, Cyril."

Cyril shrugged. "Told you I was a black sheep. Funny thing is, when I do something right nobody notices. Nobody."

"God notices," Millie said.

"Prove it," Cyril said. "Prove that He sees one bit of what I do or anything I am inside. Prove that one thing I have ever done matters to Him."

"It says in the Bible —"

"Yeah? Well, I read the Bible. I know what it says. But I want to know that God really sees me. You wouldn't understand, Millie," he said, and walked away.

Millie realized that her mouth was open but she had no words to say. She stared at Cyril as he left and thought about his comments. *Those are questions I asked myself when I was younger. They are the same questions Gavi was asking me. Is the Bible true in the same way for everyone? Are His promises for me? Does He really see what I do, and know who I am inside? It was all the same question, really. Is there a living God who cares for me? Why can't I answer them?* Millie sobbed silently to herself. *Lord, Mamma and Pappa aren't here to answer Cyril's questions and I don't think anything I say will be good enough. Please, Lord, will You speak to him? Will You show him? Show him You care.*

Trouble on Keith Hill

The excitement of taking care of the house on Keith Hill had worn off for everyone, and even Ru began to look at the calendar on the kitchen wall longingly.

"Do you think they might come early? Aunt Wealthy might have improved faster than they expected."

"They might," Millie said hopefully. "All we can do is keep the house in good order until they do."

Gavriel's cooking was still a fire hazard in the kitchen, but Millie realized that she could not have managed at all without the young woman's help with the children. Gavi had a way of kissing bruises to make them better, showing them how to share the swing, and teaching them all things about Inspiration and Glory that they never would have guessed. She seemed to fill the corners of the day when they missed Mamma the most. Millie wasn't the least surprised that Gordon was smitten with the young woman, and Millie more than suspected that Gavi felt the same way toward him.

"What are you laughing at, Millie Keith?" Gavi asked one day as they walked up the hill from a picnic by the river. Fan, Annis, and Jaz had recently decided that they were all princesses and tried to walk everywhere as if they were balancing books on their heads, which made walks and picnics a bit of a trial.

"Myself," Millie said. "Do you know that once upon a time I thought God sent you here because *you* needed help? I see His plan now — I am the one who needed help. You do realize I could not have survived these last weeks without you. I mean that with all my heart," Millie said.

"I would never have imagined you as a friend the first time I saw you, Millie Keith," Gavi said seriously. "You were so

209

stylish and poised. If you hadn't crawled out that stagecoach window, I never would have." Gavi's smile grew until it seemed to cover her whole face. "But any girl who will brave death in French lace pantalets and button-up shoes—"

"Don't forget my periwinkle cap," Millie said sadly, pretending to stifle a tear. "I never will."

"How could I forget that?" Gavi said gravely. "You do have a keen fashion sense."

"I may have fashion sense," Millie admitted, "but God looks at the heart. And when He looked at mine, He saw a girl who needed a friend."

When they reached home, Gordon Lightcap met them at the garden gate. "Princesses," he said with a bow, opening the gate for the three little girls followed by Millie and Gavi, who curtsied to him as they went through.

"Millie!" Annis tugged on Millie's skirt. "Lookit!" Millie followed the little girl's gaze. Cyril was sitting on the peak of the barn roof, his back against the pole that held the weather vane.

"Cyril!" Fan bellowed. "You had better get down from there! You might fall!" Cyril ignored her.

"Would you like me to go up and get him?" Gordon asked.

"No," Millie said, handing Gordon the basket she carried. "I'll go talk to him, if you could carry this inside."

"I'm right here if you need me," Gordon assured her, ushering the princesses up the walk after Gavi.

Millie walked all the way around the barn, but could not figure out how Cyril had climbed on top. She finally gave up, went inside, and climbed the ladder to the hayloft. The open window at the far end was just under Cyril's feet. Millie settled herself in the window with her own feet hanging out.

"Hello, Cyril," she said. "What are you doing up there?"

There was a long pause and then he said, "Thinkin'." The voice floated down as if a very depressed angel were hovering about her, just out of sight.

"I thought you went out in the rowboat with Jed and Don."

"They left me. Again." Millie could hear the grief in his voice. Don had been no more than civil to his twin brother since their fight.

"I don't think Mamma and Pappa would approve of your sitting on the barn roof," Millie said.

"Yeah? I don't guess they'd approve of much I do. When they get home, I get to tell them I was smokin' and almost got Fan killed with a lie. I'm sure lookin' forward to that, all right."

"Fan wasn't harmed," said Millie.

"But she could have drowned or been bit by a snake. Now nobody likes me. I don't have anybody to talk to anymore," he groaned.

"You could talk to Jesus," suggested Millie.

There was a long pause this time. "I've been tryin'. The words just don't come out."

Lord, help me say the right thing, Millie prayed. "Do you remember how Mamma taught us to pray?" Millie asked.

"We said the words after her," he replied.

"Well, what if I prayed and you said the words after me?"

"Let me think about it." He thought so long that Millie wanted to check and see if he'd fallen off the roof. "What if you say somethin' I don't mean?" he asked at last.

"Then you don't have to repeat it," Millie said.

"We can try," Cyril finally agreed.

211

Millie's Steadfast Love

"Jesus, I'm sorry for the things I have done that hurt You," prayed Millie. Cyril repeated the words, so low that Millie could barely hear them. "Examine my heart, Lord. I want to be right before You." She paused.

"Examine my heart, Lord," Cyril repeated. But suddenly the words started pouring out of him. "I just . . . I just want to know if You're there. Did You even see any of the stuff I've done? I know I shouldn't have been smokin' behind the woodpile, and I'm really sorry that I took that rock candy from Mr. Monocker's store." Here Millie looked up toward his dangling legs in surprise. "An' pulled the wash off Mrs. Prior's line, an' smashed the Roes' punkins so they wouldn't get bigger than Don's, an' took that dime from the offering plate, and all the other mean, low-down things I've done, an' 'specially lying to Fan. I do want to live for You, Jesus, like Mamma and Pappa. I just gotta know for sure." The flow of words stopped and Millie waited.

"Millie?" he called down to her at last. "Do you think God heard me?"

"I'm certain He did," Millie said assuredly. "Come down off the roof now, all right?"

"All right, but you gotta get out of the way."

Millie gathered her skirts and moved back into the hayloft. Cyril appeared, hanging by his arms. Millie held her breath as he swung back and forth a few times, and then launched himself into the loft.

"How did you get up there?" Millie asked as he brushed the straw from his overalls. Then she quickly added, "Never mind, I don't want to know. Just don't go up there again—"

"Until Pappa gets home," he said. "I know."

"And about that candy from the Monockers' store . . ."

"I'll tell him about it. He'll prob'ly put me to work."

~~~

When the sixth week came, the anticipation was almost unbearable.

"Will Mamma come today?" Annis asked at the breakfast table each morning. Fan spent hours in Millie's swing, pushing it as high as she could to get a better view of the road from the Lightcaps' stable, where the stagecoach would drop off her parents.

Millie and her sisters redoubled their efforts on the house, determined that it should be spotless and in order no matter what time their parents arrived. Even the Pleasant Plains Ladies Society was hard-pressed to find anything to do to help. Ru paid special attention to grooming the gardens and yards.

On Saturday morning, Ru came in from milking the cow with a worried look on his face. "I don't like the feel of the air," he said. "It feels all wrong—heavy and thick—and the dawn was awful red this morning."

By noon, a storm grumbled on the horizon and the clouds covered the sun. Millie released the boys from their lessons early to help Ru put the animals away, and with Gavi's help she shuttered the upstairs windows. By the time Belle and the horses were locked in the barn and the chicks were all shut in the henhouse, rain was falling and lightning bolts battled across the sky.

The air seemed to vibrate as all of them gathered in the kitchen. Suddenly the storm lashed out with a violence that took everyone's breath away. The wind shook the whole house, rattling the windows and tearing at the eaves. Millie was sure it was ripping shingles from the roof. There was a blinding flash and then a thunderous roar. Adah screamed.

The rain turned suddenly to hail, ice stones as large as hen's eggs smashing into the ground and bouncing against the house.

"Millie, I'm scared!" Annis cried, running to hide her face in Millie's apron.

"Come away from the window, Fan," Millie said, pulling her sister away. "Run upstairs, Cyril, you and Don, and bring blankets. We're going to cover the windows. The rest of you get into the middle of the room. Don't face the windows."

"You're afraid they will break?" Ru asked, wrapping his arms around Fan and little Jaz and turning them away from the windows.

"I don't want to take any chances," said Millie. With Gavriel and Ru's help, Millie draped the heavy blankets over the two kitchen windows, blocking out what little light the storm had let through. The hailstones were smaller now, but hitting with amazing force. Annis and Jaz huddled against Gavriel's knees as Millie and Ru lit the lamps.

"Millie, is our house going to fall down?" Fan had to shout to be heard.

"I don't think so," Millie shouted back, trying to sound sure. "Pappa built it very strong, and Jesus is taking care of us."

The first fierce wave of the storm passed and the hail turned to rain once more.

Bam! Bam! Bam! It took Millie a moment to realize that the sound was coming from outside.

"That's the henhouse door," Ru said, standing up. "I've got to close it."

"All right," Millie said after a moment. "The storm seems to have calmed. I'll get the rain slickers and go with you." The wind tore at the kitchen door as Millie pulled it shut behind them.

They could see the henhouse door smacking against the side of the building. "I thought I shut it," Ru yelled as they ran across the yard. He grabbed the door, trying to push it shut. Hail was piled in the way and he set about kicking the door free as Millie held the lantern.

She heard a strange noise over the wind and the slamming of a shutter that had come loose, and turned her head trying to figure out what it was.

"Ru," she said. "Do you hear that?"

He stopped kicking at the door and stared at her. "That roaring?" he asked.

Millie nodded. "It sounds like a locomotive coming."

"There are no trains around here," Ru said, kicking at the hail again. "It's just the wind." The sound was growing louder.

"Leave it, Ru," Millie said impatiently. "We need to get inside quickly."

"I can't leave it, the chickens will . . . " Ru looked up at her, then past her.

"*Millie!*" he said in a panicked voice. She spun around. An evil tongue stretched down from the clouds, writhing and twisting as it licked up Cyril's bees down the hill.

"Twister!" Millie yelled. She grabbed his arm and started for the house. "Get the children in the pantry! Hurry!" she shouted as they burst through the back door. Gavi must have seen the monster through the doorway behind them, and she scooped up Annis and Jaz and ran for the pantry, the others right behind her. They crowded inside and Millie pulled the door shut. The horrible roaring grew louder.

"Are we going to die?" Adah asked.

Millie fought down her own fear. "No. We're going to pray." She took Gavi's hand on one side and Ru's on the other, with the children in the middle.

"Jesus," Millie began, but the storm roared louder, as if it were trying to drown out her voice. For a moment the fear was almost too strong to bear, but Millie roared back the only Scripture that came to mind: "I am convinced that neither death nor life, neither angels nor demons, neither the present nor the future, nor any powers, neither height nor depth, nor anything else in creation, will be able to separate us from the love of God that is in Christ Jesus our Lord!"

"Save us, Lord," Ru joined. And then everyone was praying at once, shouting at the top of their voices.

"Listen!" Cyril called out above the din at last. "Stop making so much noise and listen!"

The terrible roaring was gone. Millie opened the pantry door carefully. The kitchen seemed intact, but all she could see through the window near the back door was a solid wall of rain.

"Can we come out?" Don asked.

"Yes, but stay in the kitchen," Millie said. "If we hear anything we have to go back."

Millie checked the rooms upstairs and found one broken window with rain pouring in. She hung a blanket over it to keep the water out, while Ru, Cyril, and Don gathered pillows and blankets. They made the best beds they could on the kitchen floor so they could hurry into the pantry again if necessary.

The sun was shining when Ru took down the blanket curtains the next morning, but the yard outside the window was littered with debris. There were small yellow patches here and there, like dandelions fallen in the mud. Millie followed him out into the yard before she realized what they were — poor little chicks that had drowned in the storm. They were scattered here and there, some all alone and some in groups.

"No!" Ru cried, running for the corner of the house. Millie followed him around the corner and gasped in horror. The henhouse was gone. A path of destruction cut through the garden and up to the spot where the henhouse had stood; there the path turned and went past the barn, across the pasture, and down the hill, leaving shattered, twisted tree trunks in its wake.

Bodies of hens lay all around the yard, though a few survivors pecked at the earthworms between the puddles. "Pappa trusted me to take care of them," said Ru, putting his hands to his head. "He trusted me."

"There is nothing you could have done, Ru," assured Millie. But Ru was already running to the barn. Millie followed. Belle and the horses were unharmed, though a beam from the henhouse had been driven through the barn wall. Poor Belle's udder was full and red from not being milked the night before.

Ru took the milk pail and a stool and started milking her, stopping every few strokes to wipe his eyes.

Millie enlisted the help of the younger boys in gathering the dead chicks and hens, while Fan, Annis, and Jaz sat on the porch and cried. The small corner of Ru's garden that had not been destroyed by the twister had been beaten down by hail. The fence to the pasture was gone, and patches of shingles were missing from the roof.

Gavi stood in the yard with Millie after all of the chickens had been collected.

"Now this," she said, "this is a complete disaster."

Word spread quickly through town of the trouble on Keith Hill. Most of the town had been bypassed and few suffered the damage the Keiths did. Reverend Lord organized the men to help clean up and repair the roof, and the ladies helped with the damage where water had gotten in.

On the third day after the storm Millie was helping load debris into a wagon when Zillah screamed, "Mamma!" and ran past her.

Stuart and Marcia Keith stood at the garden gate, looking at the devastation. Stuart opened the gate and Marcia gathered as many children into her arms as she could hold. "Thank God you are all safe!" she cried. "Rhoda Jane told me you were, but I just had to see you all to believe it! I'm never leaving them again, Stuart," she said. "Never!"

Everyone seemed to be talking at once, asking questions and telling about the tornado. "You're all safe, you're all safe," Marcia kept saying, tears of joy streaming down her face.

"Pappa, what about Aunt Wealthy?" Millie asked.

"She's well. It was as mild a case as the doctor had ever seen. Unfortunately, the quarantine lasts the same so we couldn't leave, even after her condition improved," said Stuart.

"Millie," Marcia said, wading through the children. "I have waited so long to hug you!"

"You should have come last week, Mamma," Adah said. "The house was so neat and clean."

Trouble on Keith Hill

"All my treasures are safe," Pappa said, taking an armful of children from his wife. "That's all that matters."

Gavi looked on from the side of the porch, Jed and Jaz standing on each side looking out with wide-eyed awe at the tender homecoming.

"You must be Gavriel," Marcia said, turning to her. "My husband has told me such good things about you. I'm thankful that you were here with Millie to help, and I want you to know that you are welcome to stay as long as you like." Gavi smiled shyly at her, but Don was already pulling on Mamma's arm, wanting to show her the tornado's path.

Stuart and Marcia stood at the point where the twister's fury had turned away from the house.

"I want to thank God right here," Stuart said, "for His faithfulness and care." He bowed his head and began to pray. The others joined him, all of them pressing in close to one another.

⸻

Millie allowed Cyril time to talk to Pappa himself, and she knew that he had done so the next day when they came down from working on the roof together. They both looked grim and a little sad. That night Millie took out the letter from Miz Opal and read it to her parents.

"Two thousand dollars is so much," she said. "I don't know how it can happen. But I believe that God spoke to me about it. I think He said that nothing is impossible with Him."

"I think you may be right," Stuart said with a twinkle in his eye. "Would you like to tell them, or shall I?" he asked Marcia.

Millie's Steadfast Love

"You tell them," Marcia said with a smile. "But please try not to be overly dramatic."

"Overly dramatic!" he said, feigning hurt feelings. "Indeed! I shall stick strictly to the facts, my dear, as always. Aunt Wealthy insisted we go to a meeting of the Friends church in Lansdale the night before we left," he explained. "The congregation listened attentively to the story of Luke and Laylie. . . "

"Told by your father," Marcia said, interrupting, "with such drama and fire that the Bard himself would have set down his quill for shame! Millie, I suspect they have declared you an angel."

" . . . *and* they took up an offering." His eyes twinkled. "Would anyone care to guess how much it is?"

"Two thousand dollars?" Don asked hopefully.

"One thousand, nine hundred, ninety-seven dollars and thirty-eight cents," Stuart said.

"How much did you say?" Cyril asked, pushing back his chair.

"One thousand, nine hundred, ninety-seven dollars and thirty-eight cents." Stuart repeated happily. "An odd number, but you never know what God is up to . . . " Stuart's voice trailed off as he looked into his son's crumpled face.

"Why, Cyril, what's wrong?" Marcia asked, starting toward him. Cyril Keith was weeping like a small child. He wiped his nose on his sleeve and went to the milk and eggs tin.

"God knew," he said, as he dumped out the change he had given Millie the first time she read the letter. "He already knew what I did. Don't you see?" He wiped his nose on his sleeve. "It's two dollars and sixty-two cents. That makes exactly two thousand!"

Trouble on Keith Hill

Stuart Keith prepared the offer to buy Luke and Laylie the next day, including instructions for the transfer of funds if the terms were accepted. "I'm sending it to Uncle Horace," he explained to Millie. "Although the children technically belong to his in-laws, I'm sure the offer will have more weight if Horace presents it."

"Do you think he will, Pappa?"

"I believe so. Horace is a good man in a very hard situation. I think he will do everything in his power to make this right. And the owners would be foolish not to take the money. Their slaves are gone, after all."

Millie carried it to the post office herself, noting that it was written as though it was from Stuart's law firm. *Thank You, Lord*, she prayed as she watched Mrs. Monocker put it in the postal satchel. *Surely it will be accepted. Hasn't God already done the impossible for Luke and Laylie? It is for freedom that Christ has set them free!* Millie felt as if creation was smiling at the incredible goodness of God, and she smiled along with it all the way home.

The stories of their adventures and family news took days to tell, mostly in the evenings after a hard day's work. Aunt Wealthy was fully recovered, it seemed, but she had hired a woman to help with the housework. All of the pox sufferers had survived, which was nothing short of a miracle. The Keith children were so eager for the presence of Stuart and Marcia that for days they seemed to move together in a group. Whether working in the house or garden, they seemed like a mass of buzzing bumblebees, gyrating around Stuart and Marcia. Gavi spent more time alone, but Jaz and Jed crept longingly to the outskirts of the group, and Marcia soon included them in the hugs and stories.

Making a home is more than keeping the children well nourished and out of trouble, Millie realized as she watched her brothers and sisters. *It's more than keeping the house clean and the washing done. I did all that. But Mamma tends her children's hearts as if they were a garden, keeping the weeds away, watering us with Jesus' love, keeping us safe while we grow. No wonder Pappa loves her so. I worried more about whether Cyril was smoking than whether his heart was set on Jesus. I cared for their physical needs, but not their hearts.* Millie's own heart hurt at the thought, but it was several days before she had a chance to share it with her mother.

Marcia listened carefully as Millie explained her pride in her housekeeping and how badly she felt she had done with the children. It was the first evening that they had been able to take a walk, just the two of them. Stuart had winked at his wife when he offered to read to the children, and Marcia had taken Millie's hand and they slipped out the door.

"You did a good job, Millie," Marcia said when Millie stopped at last. "I'm very proud of you."

"I didn't, Mamma. I know I couldn't keep the house from almost blowing down, but Cyril smoked cigars, Fan thought she was turning into a cow, Don and Cyril had a fistfight, and Zillah has fallen in love with the sheriff. All of it springs from their hearts—the very part that I was not caring for! I'm sure I'm never going to have children of my own. I'm not wise enough, and I'm afraid I never will be."

Mamma laughed. "Nonsense. The Lord in His wisdom first sends us babies—not twelve year olds. By the time you have a son who smokes cigars or a daughter in love with the sheriff, you will have had years and years of practice in training them up in the Lord, and you will be much more mature in the Lord, too."

"The worst part was questions I couldn't answer," Millie said. "Gavriel asked if the promises of the Bible are for all of us, and I didn't know how to answer her. She has had such a hard life. And Cyril—he asked me to prove that God was real. I knew the Scriptures, but . . . " She shook her head and sighed heavily.

"We can tell people about our dear Lord," Marcia said. "We can tell them what He has done, and we can show them His love. But in the end, God Himself comes to meet each of His children. He is the only one who can prove Himself, Millie."

"Like He did to Cyril," responded Millie.

"Like He did to Cyril," Marcia said with conviction. "Each of us has our own special love story with God—the story of how He proved Himself to us, how He came into our lives. I do know part of the answer for Gavriel—God's promises *are* for each and every one of His children. But I don't know the adventure He has planned for her. I only know that it will be good, because He is good."

"I think I may know part of His good plan for her," Millie said with a smile. She looked up to see Gordon Lightcap coming up the road, a bouquet in his hands.

"Good evening, ladies," he said. "May I escort you home?"

"Are those flowers for me?" Marcia teased.

"No, ma'am," Gordon said, "though I'll bring you some tomorrow, if you like. I've had a certain young lady on my mind for a while, and I'm thinking it's time I say something about it."

"I see!" Marcia smiled. "Then I suggest we go up to the house."

Everyone looked up as they came in. Gordon walked straight up to Gavi and held out the flowers. "Miss Mikolaus," he began, but he never finished the sentence. Gavi put her hands over her face and ran from the room.

"Gavi?" Millie knocked on the bedroom door Gavi had shut behind her. "May I come in? If you want to talk . . . "

"Come in," called a faint voice. Millie pushed the door open, peering cautiously around until she could see into the room. Gavi was busy throwing things into her trunk.

"Surely you're not leaving?" Millie asked, puzzled. "Gavi . . . whatever it is, we can talk about it. I . . . I truly want to be your friend. And Mamma and Pappa are eager for you to stay on with us. This is a good place for Jedidiah and Jaz; you've said so yourself. And Gordon—"

"Gordon is the reason I have to leave," Gavi said, looking up for the first time since Millie had entered the room. The haunted look had returned to her beautiful, dark eyes, and tears had gathered in them. "I could fall in love with him so easily . . . " she started, her voice catching in a sob.

"I'm sure that Gordon would love you too," Millie said, taking a step toward her friend. "You would make him so happy."

"Oh, *please* don't say that," Gavi sobbed. "Gordon Lightcap is the most wonderful man I have ever met. But I can't love him, Millie. I can't. I'm a married woman!"

Will Millie discover Gavi's dark secret at last?
Will Millie and Charles ever see each other again?

Find out in:

MILLIE'S GRAND ADVENTURE

Book Six
of the
*A Life of Faith:
Millie Keith* Series

Collect our other
A Life of Faith Products!

Beloved Literary Characters
Come to Life!

*Y*our favorite heroines, Millie Keith, Elsie Dinsmore, Violet Travilla, Laylie Colbert, and Kathleen McKenzie are now available as lovely designer dolls from Mission City Press.

*M*ade of soft-molded vinyl, these beautiful, fully-jointed 18¾" dolls come dressed in historically-accurate clothing and accessories. They wonderfully reflect the Biblical virtues that readers have come to know and love about Millie, Elsie, Violet, Laylie, and Kathleen.

For more information, visit www.alifeoffaith.com or check with your local Christian retailer.

A Life of Faith® Products from Mission City Press —

"It's Like Having a Best Friend From Another Time"